MW00769118

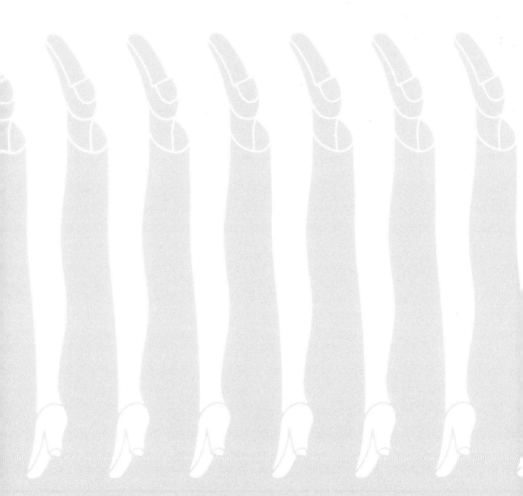

# PROVOCATEUR

Jarvid

It is great to have
you as a new friend.

Chuck

# PROVOCATEUR

A NOVEL

## CHARLES D. MARTIN

**Chaney-Hall Publishing**
Newport Beach, California

Chaney-Hall Publishing
660 Newport Center Drive, Suite 1220
Newport Beach, California 92660

This is a work of fiction. Names, characters, places and incidents either are the product of the author's imagination or are used fictitiously, and any resemblance to actual persons, living or dead, business establishments, events or locales is entirely coincidental.

First Edition

Hardcover: ISBN 978-0-9851984-0-4
Paperback: 978-0-9851984-1-1
Ebook: 978-0-9851984-2-8

*Publisher's Cataloging-In-Publication*

Martin, Charles D., 1937-
    Provocateur : a novel / Charles D. Martin. -- 1st ed. -- Newport Beach, Calif. : Chaney-Hall Publishing, c2012.

    p. ; cm.

    ISBN: 978-0-9851984-0-4 (cloth) ; 978-0-9851984-1-1 (pbk.) ; 978-0-9851984-2-8 (ebk.)

    Summary: A thriller exploring the timeless contest between men and women, looked at through the encounters of a superior, predatory, enigmatic female as she engages alpha males in the game of life.

    1. Man-woman relationships--Fiction. 2. Women--Sexual behavior-Fiction. 3. Rich people--Fiction. 4. Mail order brides--Fiction. 5. Suspense fiction. I. Title.

PS3613.A77782 P76 2012          2012907534
813.6--dc23                     1208

Image by M.C. Escher, M.C. Escher's "Fall of Man", © 2011, The M.C. Escher Company-Holland. All rights reserved. www.mcescher.com

Endsheet image by Shigeo Fukuda, © Shigeo Fukuda, "Legs of Two Different Genders", Ginza Graphic Gallery (ggg). © Photo DNP Foundation for Cultural Promotion, Shigeo Fukuda exhibition 1975, permissions granted by Shizuko Fukuda.
http://www.dnp.co.jp/gallery/ggg_e/

Printed in the United States of America on acid-free paper.

Book consultant: Ellen Reid
Cover and book design: Patricia Bacall
Author photo: Sheri Geoffreys

Fall of Man

M.C. Escher (1927)

# PROLOGUE

IN THIS NOVEL WE EXPLORE THE timeless contest between men and women. This aspect of the human experience occurs every day in our lives at all levels of the social order. In this story, we look at it through the encounters of a superior, predatory, enigmatic female as she engages alpha males, at the top of their species, in the *game of life*.

# CONTENTS

# CHAPTER 1

# PRELUDE

Gladys and Henry had just finished an elegant dinner at the exclusive, very expensive Andrea's Restaurant at the Pelican Hill Resort, just south of Newport Beach in California. Gladys needed to visit the ladies' room before the couple would begin their drive back to their home in Anaheim Hills. Knowing that it was likely to take her some time, Henry seated himself in the bar to await her return.

He noticed a very attractive young woman seated at the bar with an older well-dressed woman, perhaps her mother. She noticed him looking at her and rose from her seat, approaching him. She sat down next to him and asked,

"May I join you?"

He responded, "Of course, but I am only here for a few minutes. I'm waiting on my wife."

"Is that your mother or a friend that you are with?" Henry asked.

"She is a business associate…actually my boss," the young woman replied. "But she is busy on her cell phone, so I thought that I would come over and visit with you."

Henry was flattered. "Well, that is nice."

Henry, a moderately affluent man in his sixties, was flattered to be approached by her and for her to engage him in conversation. It had been a long time since a young woman had "hit on him." He was surprised with the young woman's forwardness but was delighted with it. She turned toward him and crossed her legs. She was wearing a short dress, and the sight of her beautiful legs was tantalizing him. It was a pleasure that took him back to his bachelor days thirty years earlier.

1

However, in the back of his mind there was a fear that Gladys would return and be angry, finding him with this young woman giving him adoring attention.

The woman spoke to him in a foreign accent that he thought might be Russian.

"I notice your watch is a Patek Philippe. You must be a connoisseur of fine things," the young woman said admiringly. "You must be a very successful man."

Her leg came in contact with his. She grasped his hand and held it up to admire the watch. The warmth of her young hand touching him caused Henry to feel a hormone rush.

Henry was a successful man by most standards. After graduating from college he was hired by a large conglomerate company. It was a good job. Over the years he gradually was promoted to increasingly more responsible positions in the company. It provided a good living, and he was able to put two children through college. They both had good jobs themselves and were raising their own families. He could feel good about that.

Henry was now recently retired and often reflected back on his life. He had always been reluctant to make changes. He had career opportunities from time to time that could have led him to higher success. But, in each case, it would have involved some risk, a risk that he did not want to take. So he had only worked for the same, big secure company all his life.

He also thought about his marriage to Gladys. He had married her young, just after his graduation from college. Getting married at that time was her idea. He did not enter the relationship with enthusiasm, but Gladys was a strong minded woman, and he acquiesced.

Gladys was of German extraction. She had grown to be a fairly stout woman and was quite domineering in her manner. Henry was actually somewhat fearful of her but didn't know why. He never was happy in the marriage, but, like with his job, he was reluctant to make a change.

Now life had passed him by. In his late sixties, he had put on some weight, and his hairline had receded considerably. Often he daydreamed about being with a young woman who adored him, one that was not constantly critical of him as Gladys was.

He thought back on his life and the many opportunities that he had passed up in his business life and with women. Why had he always been willing to just go along with what came to him? Why had he never been willing to take any chances…why had he never taken "the road less travelled?"

He was now enjoying the experience at Pelican Hill with the young woman, even though he knew her interest in him could not be genuine.

At that moment, he was jolted out of his sublime state of pleasure by Gladys, who returning from the restroom, found him in this compromising situation.

"Henry!!!" She exclaimed in a loud voice of disapproval that he knew all too well.

The young woman jumped off her chair and disappeared. Henry was lectured all the way home about how embarrassing it was for her and "What was a married man of his age doing with this young girl?" Henry heard little of his wife's ranting and raving. All he could think about was the sight of the girl's crossed legs in front of him.

When they arrived home and he was undressing to retire for the evening, he noticed that his Patek Philippe watch was gone. He had been poached on by the young woman, and Gladys was sure to notice that the watch had been stolen.

He was deflated…and in for more grief from his wife, but as he lay in bed that night, all he could think about, fanaticize about, was the memory of the warm touch of the young woman back at Pelican Hill.

The young woman was indeed Russian. Her name was Nadia. The episode at Pelican Hill was simply a training exercise. She was being groomed for bigger things. The older woman with her was Olga, her guardian and mentor…the Grande Dame of what she had come to know as *the agency*. Nadia's journey had not been an easy one, but interesting passages lay ahead.

# CHAPTER 2

# EARLY LIFE

NADIA GREW UP IN THE INDUSTRIAL city of Bryansk, Russia, near the Belarus border. She had been conceived out of the passion of two college students on a summer night along the shore of the river that ran through the town. So she had been born out of wedlock to a student that could not afford to keep her. That college student, her biological mother, asked the nurse at the hospital to name her baby "Nadia," meaning *hope* in Russia. It was an aspirational expression on the part of a mother that she would never know. It was her inauspicious entry into the world.

Nadia had lived in an orphanage in Bryansk from infancy until she entered college. Affection was a human emotion that she had rarely experienced. As a baby, she was cared for by a Russian nurse that was a strict disciplinarian. The nurse was responsible for a great number of infants, and Nadia was just one of them. She never held Nadia or touched her in a caring way. Perhaps because of that, Nadia tended to be somewhat disconnected from others and struggled with the emotion of love.

In the orphanage, living conditions were terrible. Generally eight to ten children slept on a mattress on the floor; nutrition was poor, and there was little heat in the building. She and others in the orphanage suffered neglect and abuse. There were simply too many unwanted children for the facility and staff to absorb. In order to keep order in the orphanage, workers would severely discipline the children.

Children came into the orphanage from many sources. Some, like Nadia, were babies given up by mothers that could not afford to raise them. But many were older children that had been abandoned by poor parents or left behind as a result of divorce. Frequently there were gypsy-like children that were placed in the orphanage by police after being picked up on the streets. Often they had no schooling, and some had never developed language skills. They would communicate with each other by making strange sounds—a primitive language that had evolved on the streets. In the orphanage, children of all ages were mixed together, but at age sixteen they had to leave.

The staff was poorly paid and overworked, and the work was stressful because the children were unruly and difficult to manage. Consequently, there was a lot of turnover. Rarely did one of the social workers stay on the job for more than a year. This meant that they never got to know any of the children personally or develop any caring relationships. In most orphanages, the ratio of staff to children was more than thirty to one.

Nutrition was also poor. With very little financial resources, the children's diet consisted mostly of bread, soup, and sometimes a thin gruel with tiny morsels of pale, tasteless meat. Nadia grew very thin during her youth. The gypsy children would often steal the food of others. Days were very regimented, with children being herded like prisoners between the dining areas, play areas, and sleeping areas. All were required to do work around the facility. Children were seldom allowed outside for fear that they would run away.

Under these bleak and hopeless conditions, the orphans developed strange behaviors. No one smiled. There was nothing to be happy about. A smile would seem fake, insincere; so when one looked at the faces of the children, all were contorted in frowns. There always seemed to be a profound sadness to them. None would look another in the eye when speaking to another orphan, social worker, or visitor. Eye contact was considered a rude or an aggressive action. They all looked down or away when greeting or talking to another.

Children were often subjected to beatings, and sexual abuse was common. Nadia tried to remain inconspicuous to avoid being targeted by the male workers. She was skinny and made herself as unattractive as she could in other ways. While this helped, she could not avoid the advances of the men workers entirely, especially as she grew older.

Sometimes there were small groups of people that would visit the orphanage from other nations. These were mostly church missions. They would bring food, clothes, and a few well-worn books. They cared about the children and were appalled with the conditions that they lived in, but they came and left, rarely to be heard from again.

Occasionally, the orphanage would be visited by a couple seeking to adopt a child. This was an exciting time, filling Nadia with hope that she would get chosen. Virtually all of these were foreigners. It seemed that they only wanted babies, so there was no opportunity for older children to escape the miserable life in the orphanage. Nadia's hopes of adoption eventually disappeared.

In the orphanage, many children did not even have names. Their circumstances of abandonment on the streets or being born out of wedlock and given up at the hospital meant that the official government records did not contain any information on their identities. To the government—and to the world at large—it was as if they were non-persons.

A nurse had given Nadia her name in the maternity ward at the hospital, but she had no family name for years. Eventually, she needed a last name for her school, so Nadia chose the name "Borodin" after Alexander Borodin, one of the great Russian composers. Although no government records reflected it, from that point forward she claimed the name "Nadia Borodin."

For Nadia to survive in this environment she had to be resourceful, using her cleverness to avoid hunger and abuse. She learned how to manipulate other orphans and the caregivers at the facility. She schemed to win the favor of a few key older, stronger children, so they would protect her from the aggressive gypsy children and provide her a warm place to sleep at night. During the winter, because the build-ing had no heat, many children caught severe colds or pneumonia.

Bryansk is a thousand-year-old Russian provincial city of about 400,000 poor souls. It is located on the banks of the Desna River about one hundred kilometers equidistant from Belarus and the Ukraine. It is mainly an industrial city known for its steel works and machinery manufacturing. Its economy also has an element of garment production and agriculture.

 The city is populated by ancient churches that exemplify the classic Slavic architecture of the pre-Soviet period. But mostly the city is comprised of drab gray buildings with plain boxy archi-tecture, typical of those built during the Communist era. Their dingy sameness pervades the entire city. Very few people live in homes in Bryansk; most are housed in tenement-style apart-ment buildings that have suffered from a lack of maintenance for decades. Likewise, schools, universities, and government buildings are all simple gray structures.

The city has a good system of trolleys that provide public transpor-tation. On the roads one sees mainly old, inexpensive cars and many rickety old trucks of all kinds transporting goods between Russia and the Ukraine or Belarus. Roads and buildings are essentially all run-down and dirty. Summers can be pleasant in the countryside that surrounds the city, but winters are severe.

At the orphanage most of the other children were so education-ally deprived and backward that there was little reason for Nadia to interact with them. She felt isolated, alone. As a result she turned inward, retreating into her own mind for intellectual stimulation. Consequently, she became introverted.

For Nadia, there was one thing that kept her going. She had an unquenchable thirst to learn. It was a passion for her … and an escape. School was not enough for her. When the orphanage administration would allow, she would go to the Bryansk Public Library and read for hours. There was no subject that did not interest her. All aspects of the world captivated her. Through her reading, her mind could take her to far-off places vicariously and to experiences that were beyond anything she expected to enjoy in her lifetime.

Often she would lose track of time in the solitude of the library and her engagement with the content in the books. Returning to the orphanage late, she was certain to be punished.

Nadia enjoyed school. In Russia, schooling was compulsory and free through the senior secondary level (grade 11). Learning was easy for her … very easy. She had been genetically endowed with a beautiful mind. While other students in the classroom struggled to memorize the material or grasp complex concepts, her intellectual engagement with the material provided a crystal-clear pathway into her mind. Weeks later, in the course of an exam, she could recall the image on the chalkboard where the teacher had outlined information that was to be on a test. Mentally, she could again see it in every detail, like a photograph.

Literature and other subjective subjects that involved an emotional quotient were a little more difficult for her, but subjects of an objective nature, such as mathematics and science, came easy. In her schooling, she had success. Although she appeared at school in tattered cloths and was known to be an orphan, a number of her teachers recognized her exceptionalness and encouraged her. This gave her a boost of self-confidence and a positive experience that she had nowhere else in her life.

As a young teenager, she physically developed early. This made her a target for the men that worked in the orphanage. Given an opportunity, they would molest her and seek further gratification. But she was successful in avoiding their more aggressive advances, although she lived under a constant fear of rape.

Because of her scholastic achievement, one teacher, Ms. Lynski, took a particular interest in her. Ms. Lynski was aware of the hardships faced by children in the orphanage. She was a caring person in this otherwise desolate place.

After school one day, she talked to Nadia.

"Soon you will be graduating from secondary school. You are a bright young lady and should continue your education at the university. Upon graduation from secondary school, you will no longer be able to live at the orphanage."

Ms. Lynski paused and added, "I know a nice couple who might be willing to take you in. They are both professors at the Bryansk State University and have no children of their own. While they would have no interest in adoption, they have a spare room in their apartment and have an interest in bright young people. They had another girl living with them, but she graduated from the university and recently got married. Perhaps they would be interested in you."

Nadia beamed. "That would be wonderful! I have nowhere else to go."

"Would you like me to ask them for you?" Ms. Lynski offered. "It would be a much better environment than the orphanage."

"I can't stay in the orphanage. They have told me that I must leave. I would like very much for you to ask them," Nadia said with hopeful anticipation. "Please inquire on my behalf. What are their names?"

"Dmitri and Lara Ivanhov," Ms. Lynski replied.

The Ivanhovs were friends of Ms. Lynski, so her inquiry was well received. She arranged for Nadia to meet the Ivanhovs, and her interview session went well.

Dmitri Ivanhov described the arrangement that they would offer.

"Nadia, we would be delighted to bring you into our home, but you must understand the arrangement. Lara and I both have our positions at the university, so you must help us by doing much of the housework around our apartment. You will also need to get a part-time job and reimburse us a small amount for some of your food and other expenses.

"Another thing," Dr. Ivanhov continued. "You are not allowed to bring boys to our home, you cannot do any drugs or alcohol, and you must always be on good behavior. If you drop out of school or violate these rules, we will require that you leave."

"I am grateful for the opportunity, and you will have no problem with me," Nadia said.

Dr. Ivanhov nodded. "Fine, then it is agreed, and you can move in when you wish."

Nadia was elated. She packed up her meager belongings and moved into the Ivanhovs' apartment, embarking on a very positive phase of her life. She had just graduated from secondary school and entered college at the Bryansk State University. Nadia got a night-shift job in a garment manufacturing company and would take classes during the daytime. She would catch up on sleep when she could and was diligent about taking care of her duties around the Ivanhov household.

The Ivanhovs were good to her and provided a vibrant intellectual environment in which she could grow. Years went by, and while she lived a modest lifestyle, it was without the spirit-breaking hardship of the orphanage. It was a difficult schedule, so she had no social life. At the university she had met other girls, but no close relationships developed. As an orphan, other students mostly shunned her. She was never seen with boys. Her detachment issues and unpleasant encounters with men made her cautious about relationships with the opposite gender.

All of this made for a lonely life for Nadia. While she was highly intelligent, she was very introverted and had no financial means to participate in activities with other students. Yes, it was a lonely life, but it was a step up from the survival mode that she had existed in for all of her younger years.

She often wondered about her biological mother and father. They probably lived in Bryansk and perhaps had gone to the Bryansk Public University. They would be about the same age as Dmitri and Lara. *Perhaps they are my parents?* she thought. The whimsical notion amused her, but she quickly dismissed that possibility since the Ivanhovs' background did not line up with the time of her birth. Nevertheless, it was a pleasant thought on which to speculate. Nadia had made other efforts to track down her biological parents, but the records had all been lost.

Eventually, Nadia was to graduate and face the end of her arrangement with the Ivanhovs. It was a time just following the Russian financial crisis (the so-called Ruble Crisis of 1998) and the country was in a deep recession. The garment manufacturing company where she had worked during her college years had gone bankrupt and closed, so she had no income at all. In her field of computer science, the dot-com "bubble" had burst, and the information technology industry was in crisis. There were no jobs for college graduates, particularly in her field. What jobs were available were for laborers and tradesmen. Mostly, those jobs were for men. She had to leave the Ivanhovs' home but had no place to go.

When it came time for Nadia to move out, it was difficult emotionally. For the first time in her life she had a somewhat normal home life. She had grown to like and respect the Ivanhovs, and they had grown to have an affection for her. However, years before, Dmitri and Lara made a mutual decision that they would not let their live-in scholars become dependent on them … or let themselves become so attached to the students that they would not rotate out graduates and bring in new students starting their education at the university. So it was a sad day when Nadia had to leave.

Nadia was desperate. She had no money, no family, and no way to live on her own. Soon the harsh Russian winter would be setting in. She feared being on the street without food or shelter, as were many others from the orphanage that had no place to go and no one to care for them.

There was a steel worker named Boris that was attracted to her and had dated her a few times. He was in his early forties and had a good job. Knowing Nadia's situation, he proposed that she marry him. Having no other options, she reluctantly agreed. Nadia would move into his modest apartment and begin her duties as a wife.

Boris was a heavy drinker. It was typical of him to stop at a bar with his male co-workers after leaving the steel mill. After too many vodkas he would stagger into their shabby apartment drunk, demanding sex. He was dirty from the mill, and his body was covered with sweat, and his breath smelled of alcohol. This was a big turn-off for Nadia, and she would lock herself in the bedroom to avoid his advances. He would get angry and kick down the door. He would abuse her and have his way with her. He was strong, and she could not defend herself from him. She would let her mind wander back the pleasant days with the Ivanhovs when she was secure from such incursions by aggressive males.

However, the marriage provided something for each of them. He provided a living, and she took care of their home and prepared their meals every day. He had his carnal desires fulfilled.

Nadia was not happy; she felt trapped in a bad situation from which there was no escape.

# CHAPTER 3

# SARAH'S RING

DURING HER COLLEGE DAYS, NADIA HAD developed a friendship with a girl named Sarah. Sarah was the only other student to have an affinity for Nadia, to find something in common with her. Most of Nadia's schoolmates did not socialize with her; she was a bit of an outcast. Even in the poor city of Bryansk, Nadia was at the bottom of the social order—impoverished, with no parents or family. Perhaps there was a little jealousy factor also in that Nadia always got good grades … essentially perfect grades. Other students could not understand how this poor orphan wearing dowdy clothes could do so well. They were suspicious. Because she worked after school, Nadia also could not participate in any activities with the other students. Nadia had become accustomed to being shunned by others, but she had accepted this role in her life.

The absence of experiencing affection in her young life had left Nadia disconnected emotionally from others. Because of that, she did not seek to establish social relationships.

But for some reason Sarah had empathy for Nadia and reached out to her in a gesture of friendship. After graduation and her marriage to Boris, Nadia had more time to spend with Sarah and began to develop her first real emotional attachment. In the last year of college, Sarah had become pregnant and had a child. Still she found time, about once each week, to get together with Nadia. Sarah was miserable in her own marriage. Like Boris, her husband was chauvinistic and abusive. But for her, there was no way out. Her parents, who were very poor, lived in Bryansk, and burdened with a child, she could not escape her circumstances.

Unhappiness was something they shared. Sarah escaped the drudgery of her real life by venturing into cyberspace, visiting regularly an Internet café near where she and Nadia would meet for lunch. Her journey in cyberspace was a way of vicariously experiencing a better life, of traveling to faraway places. She would tend to fantasize a lot. They often talked about the many challenges and disappointments that they shared with how their lives were going. Sarah took Nadia to the Internet café one day and showed her some of the sites that she enjoyed visiting.

"One of my friends has told me about a website that places Russian girls with wealthy husbands in America," Sarah said. "I have had fun exploring it. Let me show you."

"How interesting!" Nadia replied, craning her head over Sarah's shoulder to view the computer screen as Sarah navigated to the site. "It would be a dream to live in America, to have some financial security and perhaps a caring husband."

The two of them toured the site and did so again when they met the following week. It was intriguing but also somewhat disheartening, as there were seemingly countless Russian women seeking American husbands.

Despite the competition, Nadia thought, *Perhaps this is a way out of my dismal life here in Bryansk.*

She and Sarah talked about it a lot. If Boris ever found out that she had registered on the site he would be furious. There was no telling what he might do to her. She reassured herself with the knowledge that Boris had no computer skills and could not find out.

"Nadia, you should do this. Boris will never know, and perhaps you can find a good man in America," Sarah insisted.

"I will try it, but it must be a secret—just between the two of us!" Nadia replied anxiously.

"Absolutely!" pledged Sarah.

Nadia signed up for the mail-order-bride program and began to correspond with men who made inquiries on the site. Several weeks went by, and she had growing traffic on her page on the site. Nadia and Sarah enjoyed the process, daring to dream that something positive might happen, although it seemed a remote possibility.

In the course of the registration, Nadia provided cleverly worded information about herself and an attractive photo. She was silent about the fact that she was married. Since the Internet company was the go-between on contacts with bride seekers, all information exchanged was confidential, and it was not necessary for her to provide any home address or telephone contact information. She could remain somewhat anonymous, except for her Internet identity.

Nadia continued to return to the Internet café regularly and was developing a number of "suitors." Sarah enjoyed following along with her in the process. At some point an e-mail message came in from a woman named Kassandra who claimed to run the site and the related placement service. Kassandra indicated that she had been following Nadia's activities on the site and was also impressed with Nadia's academic accomplishments. She suggested that Nadia consider a suitor in California that had been actively pursuing her.

California sounded like a dream place, and she was excited about the prospect of living there. She had seen pictures of it in books: swaying palm trees, the azure blue of the vast Pacific Ocean, Hollywood and its glamorous movie stars with perfect hair, perfect smiles, and perfect lives. Or so Nadia believed.

The electronic dialog with the California suitor had progressed for several weeks. *Then came the proposal:* he wanted her to marry him! He would send her an airline ticket and would make all the arrangements through the mail-order-bride firm. A courier for the company would deliver a package for her to the Internet café, and a car would pick her up there and take her to the airport at Moscow. In the package would be her airline tickets, a passport that reflected her new identity, and all the necessary documents for her to leave the country. Nadia was suitably impressed; this mail-order-bride firm seemed to have exceptional connections and the means to get impossible things done.

She accepted with enthusiasm, anticipation … and some apprehension.

On the day of her departure she met with Sarah to say goodbye. They met at the Internet café where the car was to come later to pick up Nadia and take her on the long drive to the Domodedovo Airport at Moscow.

The girls talked about Nadia's hope for a new life in a far-off land.

Sarah's voice was full of hope. "Nadia, I am happy that you have chosen to take this leap into the unknown. It takes courage. You have exceptional abilities, and perhaps in America you will be able to employ those gifts to make a better life."

"I wish you could go with me," Nadia said sadly.

"That would be wonderful. But I have a child and aging parents here. I have responsibilities and cannot leave," Sarah said regretfully.

Nadia was apprehensive about her big move into the unknown and did not want to leave her only friend. "Of course, I understand. I was just dreaming for a moment and fearing, a bit, going alone to a place that I do not know and living with people that are very different."

Sarah grasped her finger, where she wore a ring that Nadia had noticed since their friendship began. She pulled it off and extended it toward Nadia.

"This ring was given to me by my grandmother. I would like you to have it."

"No! No! I can't accept a gift like that. You do not have very much yourself. It has sentimental family value. It would be too big a sacrifice for you."

Nadia gazed at the ring Sarah proffered. It was small but beautiful, with a raspberry red garnet stone set in a rose-gold band that was common many years ago in Russia when they used a copper alloy with the gold.

"I have admired it on you since we first met," she said. "Sarah, that is a wonderful gesture of friendship, but you must keep it—it is too precious."

"It would mean a lot to me if you would take it," Sarah persisted. "It is a way that I can travel with you into the new world and be connected to you in your journey into a new life."

"What a beautiful thought," Nadia said as tears welled in her eyes.

"My grandmother purchased it from a gypsy who told her that whoever wears the ring would be protected from harm and also experience good luck," Sarah explained. "As you travel off into unknown territory and life with strangers, the ring will be your protector and a way for you to remember me."

Sniffing back tears, Nadia hugged her friend and said, "Sarah, you are the only person that has cared about me. I know how precious this ring is. I will accept it and wear it proudly as a way for you to continue with me in my life."

Nadia slipped the ring on. It was a perfect fit and would become her most treasured possession. In fact, it was her *only* possession other than the clothes that she wore.

Outside the Internet café, the car had arrived to take Nadia to Moscow. She and Sarah exchanged goodbyes. Nadia noticed Sarah's chin begin to quiver and saw a tear run down her cheek. This was the first person that had sincere affection for her and she was leaving her behind. Nadia knew she would not see her again. The thought filled her with numbing sadness. She opened the car door and entered, waving to Sarah as the car pulled away. There was no turning back now.

On the long three-hour ride to the Moscow airport, Nadia was reflective. She often looked at the simple, inexpensive, but beautiful garnet ring. She hoped that the gypsy was right in her prophecy.

Nadia did not leave a note for Boris. Because of his uncaring ways, he did not even know about her friendship with Sarah.

That day, when he came home to his apartment, she was not there and she would not thereafter show up. He became frustrated and angry. The dishes were not done, and she was not there, to attend to his wishes. He contacted the police and filed a missing person's report. They speculated that she might have simply run away. Boris

SARAH'S RING | 19

knew she had no money and was totally dependent on him. *Where could she have gone?* he wondered. With no passport and no money she could not have left the country. Furthermore, in Russia, subjects are not allowed to leave the country without obtaining a permit, which was very difficult. Nadia would not have had a way to obtain the necessary documents. It was perplexing to him, and he would never know what happened to her.

Nadia had simply disappeared from Bryansk and made the journey to California to begin her new life.

# CHAPTER 4

# COMING TO AMERICA

NADIA'S DESPERATE EFFORT LED TO HER journey to America and a marriage to a plumbing contractor named Bert Cameron. Bert was a good provider but not really affluent. He lived in Encino, California, and, while not a center of wealth, to Sarah it was a paradise compared to Bryansk. Bert pursued the mail-order-bride strategy because he was aging and had never been successful with women.

Nadia had studied some languages, but her English language skills were weak. The communication challenge and age difference made for a marriage of convenience, but not a happy one. Bert, unlike her Russian husband, was an affable and decent man, always good to her. However, his business was not going well, and there was a lot of stress in the life between them.

One day Nadia received a call from a woman who introduced herself as Olga Petrovna. Olga explained that she was affiliated with the Russian website company that had placed her in America. She was following up to see how their clients were doing. Olga persuaded Nadia to meet for lunch.

At their lunch meeting, Olga questioned Nadia extensively on how things were going, and if she was happy in the relationship. The line of questioning seemed a bit odd to Nadia, but she confessed that she was only in the marriage because she had no choice. She had no family, no friends, and no means of support and could not leave her American husband.

"I trade him sex and companionship, and he provides a living for me," Nadia admitted. Her English was passable, but still spoken with a thick Russian accent.

Olga looked critically at Nadia across the table. She was wearing an inexpensive dress that did not fit well. Her hair looked like she had cut it herself, and she was not wearing any make-up or jewelry, except for a small, inexpensive garnet ring. However, Olga could see that beneath the surface was a young woman that, with a little work, could be very attractive. Also, she knew a lot more about Nadia than she let on.

Nadia stood at about five-feet-seven- or eight-inches tall and had raven black hair, straight in a bob, cut with every strand of hair in perfect place. She had those big, deep-blue eyes but not sky blue like most. Her eyes were a rich, French blue color that was piercingly beautiful. Her eyebrows were thicker than most women's. Her skin color was light, but with some subtle olive tones reflecting the possibility that she had some Asian blood mixed with her Slovak genes. Her skin was like porcelain, without a noticeable blemish anywhere. Nadia's body was in perfect proportions but without extreme voluptuousness. It displayed a more subtle contour of sensuality.

"Nadia, do you know what your name means?"

"Yes, I do. It means 'hope' in Russian … but I think it strange because I have none."

"If you want a better life and are willing to do what is necessary to get it, I can help you," Olga said.

"Olga, I have already led a life of doing what is necessary just to survive." Nadia's voice was a bit gravelly, which seemed inconsistent with her fragile appearance.

"I can provide you with an opportunity to live well, to have some financial security and interesting experiences," Olga reassured her with a subtle smile. "To do this, you must learn a new set of skills, and I must prepare you for a unique career."

"Career? What would you have me do?" Nadia said suspiciously, concerned that Olga might be proposing something illicit.

"I operate an enterprise where young women, like you, are engaged in a variety of assignments that allow us to extract large amounts of money from wealthy men," Olga said.

"Are you suggesting that I become a … a prostitute?" said Nadia slowly, uneasy about what Olga was proposing.

"No, not really … at least in the normal sense," Olga assured her.

"Would I have to do anything illegal or marry these men?" Nadia asked. "I would not like to do anything that might get me deported. I can't go back to Russia!"

Olga laughed. "You do not have to marry the men that we target or do anything that you feel uncomfortable doing. However, some of the assignments that women in my organization pursue do require a certain amount of, shall we say, nefarious conduct in order to accomplish our financial objectives."

Olga took Nadia's silence as an invitation to continue.

"I run a very special 'post graduate' program for young Russian women that want a better life. In this program, you will perfect your English language skills, learn etiquette, and my staff will groom you and enhance your beauty. You will need to become knowledgeable about many things: for example, the arts, business, and world affairs, so you can become a good companion to wealthy men. I will guide you from there on how to benefit from all of this. But I caution you, it is a long process and will take work and commitment on your part."

Olga could not help noticing that Nadia rarely made eye contact with her during their conversation. Her eyes often looked down or looked away as they talked.

"Do you lack self-confidence?" Olga asked.

"Why do you think that?" Nadia replied.

"When we speak, you do not look at me. It's generally a sign of modesty, insecurity, or a feeling of inadequacy that causes such behavior."

"I *am* insecure," Nadia said in a subdued tone. "It is also a habit that I picked up as a child, because in the orphanage looking directly at another person was interpreted as an open act of aggression. It invited hostility from the other kids. I always sought to avoid it."

"Well, Nadia, we will need to work on that," Olga responded sympathetically. "We will need to build your self-confidence. Look at me!"

Nadia lifted her eyes and stared at Olga.

Olga smiled. "You have beautiful eyes. They are incredibly unique. I have never seen such a rich blue color. They can be one of your greatest attributes. You need to learn to use them to your advantage. All that will come in the course of my work with you."

"Why me?" Nadia asked. "There are many younger, more beautiful Russian women to choose from."

"A younger, perfect female specimen would be suspect by a sophisticated, affluent male," Olga explained. "I need a more believable woman that can be more stealth-like; one that does not raise suspicion by the targeted male. A more beautiful, younger woman would be good for a one-night stand or perhaps for a week in St. Tropez … but you may have the potential for bigger things."

Olga's proposition sounded intriguing but perhaps a little shady. Nadia had no idea what she had planned for her. It was a path into the unknown, but Olga was very convincing.

As Nadia stole furtive glances at Olga, she couldn't help but wonder about her. Olga looked to be pushing sixty, but had retained her trim figure and carried herself with a cosmopolitan sophistication. In her manner, her voice, and her confidence, it was clear she was a worldly woman.

Nadia could not help notice the extravagant pink sapphire ring and art deco diamond bracelet that she wore. Her nails and hair were meticulously groomed, and she exuded a sense of class. This was a woman of charm and elegance, but from her demeanor Nadia suspected she was also one very strong-minded lady.

*How had she gotten to this place in life?* Nadia wondered.

Olga proposed that Nadia join what the others in her organization called *the agency* and pursue a path to a better, but unconventional, lifestyle. Nadia listened in fascination as Olga gradually painted a picture where Nadia would leave her husband and enter an education and personal development program that would prepare her to make a lot of money targeting wealthy, unsuspecting men. Olga claimed to know exactly how to do it. She had an elaborate set of schemes to extract money from these "targets" and had been doing so for years. As part of her enterprise she had developed access to the higher social circles in the Southern California region—and beyond, as Nadia would later learn.

As a front for this operation, Olga operated a corporate and charity event management business: *The Beverly Hills Events Management Company.* This provided an abundant supply of high-level contacts and relationships for her, as well as a platform for employing her "students" while they were in training.

Nadia raised an inquisitive eyebrow and asked, "So if I leave the security of my marriage and join your 'agency,' what would my arrangement be with you?"

Olga outlined the terms of her proposed arrangement. "I get thirty five percent of the income that you bring in for the rest of your life. You can leave *the agency* anytime you wish, but because I will remake you into a high income producer, my claim goes on forever. And, if you leave, you must also reimburse me for the investment I have made in you. Another fifteen percent goes into a pool that is shared by *the agency's* staff that supports you, allocated to the other agents in my organization, and to cover overhead expenses. You get the remaining fifty percent."

"But where would I live? I have no money to rent an apartment," Nadia protested.

Olga waved a dismissive hand. "Not to worry. I have a big house in Malibu where many of my girls live. You can stay there, and I will take care of you until you complete your first assignment and become self-sustaining."

For Nadia, it was not a difficult decision to leave her drab lifestyle and husband that she did not love. So the arrangement was struck. The divorce proceedings were simple. Nadia left the marriage with nothing, but she had gained her US citizenship through the marriage process. Olga took care of everything.

So it was that Nadia moved into the big house in Malibu and began her job at the *Beverly Hills Events Management Company*. The company was a full service events management firm that would provide rentals, catering, and entertainment for charity and corporate events in the region. Initially, her job was very menial. She worked on the installation of party rental items, dinner place settings, and floral arrangements at the sites for charity events.

The big house in Malibu was where all of the new girls lived as well as some others back from "field assignments." At any one time there were about a dozen women living "in residence" at the house. Olga insisted on tight controls over the women in her *agency*. It was a very tight-knit collection of exceptional women. Nadia heard about others that were part of *the agency* but were living somewhere outside of the house. These were the more advanced "students" that were part of Olga's *agency*.

Olga's house in Malibu was not on the beach. Rather, it perched majestically on the hillside, commanding a breathtaking panoramic view of the Pacific. It was large Mediterranean home with many bedrooms, common areas, and a swimming pool. It was what Nadia had imagined a sorority house might be like in America.

Nadia was assigned a roommate named Alexandra, or Alex as many of the girls in the house called her. Alexandra was in her mid-twenties but had been in *the agency* for many years. She had been tasked by Olga to mentor Nadia and bring her along on *the program*. Alexandra was the archetypical striking Russian beauty: a tall, lanky, blue-eyed blonde. She had come to America through the same website-operated, mail-order-bride program. Nadia would learn a lot from Alexandra and would develop a friendship with her.

After dinner on her first night in the Malibu house, Nadia and Alexandra sat in their room and talked for hours. They had a good-sized room to share. It had two full size beds, two chairs, and a desk that doubled as a vanity when they were both getting ready at the same time. They shared a small bath, but it had a shower and a tub.

"I grew up in a small town north of St. Petersburg in Russia, near the Finland border," Alexandra explained. "As a teenager, I wanted to pursue a career in modeling. In Russia I could not make any progress on my ambitions. My parents were very poor and unable to help. I thought if I could get to America, I might be able to enjoy some success.

"When I discovered Olga's mail-order-bride program, I thought it might offer a way for me to escape Russia and pursue my dream."

"Why did you come to LA instead of New York?" Nadia asked.

"Quite frankly, it was not the best choice for my modeling ambitions. But I had had enough of cold weather in Russia, especially in the far north where I lived. Hollywood and the glamour of southern California had its appeal."

"So Olga recruited you also?" Nadia asked.

"Yes, and I am happy she did," she responded.

Alexandra was a very animated and enthusiastic girl, unlike Nadia, who was quiet and reserved. There was vivaciousness about her. As she talked she would swing her head from side to side, flipping her generous blonde hair across her head in a spontaneous gesture.

"Like you, I married a man here," said Alexandra. "I lied about my age and came here as a teen. Olga was quick to extricate me from that situation. I guess she didn't want to leave me unsupervised at my young age. Anyway, there were very few modeling jobs in LA."

Nadia looked at Alexandra sitting on the edge of the bed in their room. She was a real beauty, perhaps with a combination of Russian and Scandinavian heritage. Nadia thought that she could have been a very successful model.

"You have all the attributes that were necessary to be a professional model: the height, the look, and wow—a fabulous figure."

Alex smiled at the compliment. "I did not realize it at the time, but the competition was very intense for the few modeling jobs that were available in LA, and my American husband had no connections that could get me started in the industry. It all worked out in the end, and I am very happy that Olga found me."

"There must be hundreds of Russian women that traffic Olga's web site. Why did she select us?" Nadia asked.

Alexandra sat quietly for a moment and continued. "Kassandra, who you probably also talked to in Russia, is an ex-Olga agent. She runs the mail-order-bride program and does a lot of research on the young women that become involved with the program. From the many that register on the site, they select only the best and those they believe have exceptional potential as agents. You and I are among the lucky few!" she said, bouncing up and down on the edge of her bed. "Olga's people handled everything for me, including the divorce procedure … and gave me a job at the events management company."

Nadia did not want to talk about her background—her history in Bryansk, her experience as an orphan. It was a painful part of her past that she was only now beginning to escape from.

Sensing this, Alexandra said, "Olga has given me a complete rundown on your background. You had it rough in your young years. It must also be difficult growing up without any parents … any family at all. Olga said that you have a lot going for you. She asked me to help bring you along as best I can—to help you with some of the basics to prepare you to conduct your assignments. We will have fun together.

"For me the process was easy," she continued. "In the months and years after I joined the organization, I learned Olga's ways and became a successful agent in the enterprise. I started to earn very good money, much better than I would have as a model."

It had been a big day for Nadia and she was getting tired.

"Alexandra, it was great getting to know a little about you, but I am ready to turn in." She yawned. "We have a lot to do tomorrow."

Alexandra was accustomed to staying up late but considering Nadia's wishes agreed to call it a night.

As Nadia lay there in her comfortable bed, pulling the covers up over her, she felt a calmness that she had rarely experienced. Perhaps, in this new life, she had a "family" that might care about her and some security. Perhaps, as Olga had said, she was starting down the path to a better life.

In the morning Alexandra and she went down to the kitchen and continued their talk over coffee and a continental breakfast.

"I like living here in the Malibu house," Alexandra said. "I have the means to get a place of my own, but I enjoy the camaraderie of the people on Olga's organization. I have been running mid-level missions for years and have prospered from them. My assignments have also enabled me to have fabulous experiences. Olga has told me that she believes that you have the potential for assignments that would pursue really big objectives. She asked me to teach you everything I can."

"I have a lot to learn, so I appreciate anything you can do," Nadia said. "I have no idea what Olga's assignments might involve. But I am a fast learner."

Nadia had never met a sophisticated man or had any experience with matters related to affluent people. Unlike her, Alexandra had a lot of experience with men. She knew how to handle them. She did not finish college in Russia but had developed many valuable skills. Among those, Alexandra was a very good judge of people.

Her missions had provided her the opportunity to travel and meet interesting people. She could afford beautiful clothes and jewelry. The work was not hard, and she had a good life.

Alexandra knew how to please men and make them want to do nice things for her. Her closet was jammed with beautiful clothes.

"Do you have any special man friend that you are romantically involved with?" Nadia asked.

"Over the years, I have had many romances," Alexandra sighed. "In some cases I even developed an affection for some of Olga's 'targets.' I am a hopeless romantic and love men … every aspect of them!

"Eventually, it always seemed to come to the point where my male love interest would want me to leave Olga's firm and become a wife." Alexandra paused. "None ever really knew what I did. They were content to believe that I worked for the *Beverly Hills Event Management Company*.

"When faced with the prospect of marriage, I always backed away. I was reluctant to give up my exciting way of life. I like my independence. Someday... I will get married, but I am still young so not now."

Nadia asked her how she felt about taking advantage of the men. She explained that initially it had bothered her, but over time she had become comfortable with the experience. Alexandra explained that she "sold pleasure," not as a "'lady of the night" but in a more sophisticated, covert way. Her targets would receive lasting value in the form of wonderful memories of their time together … even though, through her schemes, it would cost them a lot of money.

"Hah! They have too much money anyway," Alex rationalized.

Early in Alexandra's own "education," Olga had hired some "professionals" to teach her some of the technical skills in order to deliver a heightened pleasurable experience to her men. Alex had become a master of her trade. However, she learned that great experiences extended beyond the physical aspect of an encounter. Alexandra enjoyed getting into a man's head and exploring his whole psyche. She had also come to appreciate that there was a wide variety of men. She liked experiencing all aspects of every one of them in great depth.

All this was fun for her.

"In addition to what I learned from Olga's 'professional consultants,' I learned a lot from this book that she gave me," Alexandra said, picking up a copy of the *Kama Sutra* from her nightstand. "You can borrow it for a while. The *Kama Sutra* is an ancient Hindu treatise on sexual pleasure and the nature of love. It is both philosophical and practical."

"I am a little uncomfortable in this area," Nadia replied. "But, if you think I need to know it, I will read the book."

Alex handed her the book. Nadia leafed through it, astounded at the variety of sexual positions it presented. She sat the book on her nightstand and asked, "Alex, what about you? You must have family back in Russia. Do you miss them?"

"Yes I do, but I could never go back. I have been fortunate to do well here. So I am able to send them money. I don't know what they would do without it. Things are pretty bad there. I have a younger brother who lives with my parents. He is very sick and needs constant medical care."

"Considering all that, you seem to have a good attitude about life," Nadia observed.

Alex shrugged. "I have a good life here. California and Olga have been good to me. You will also make a better life here for yourself. Put all your past behind you, and make a fresh start."

"Olga seems like a very interesting lady. Can you tell me more about her?" Nadia asked, changing the subject.

"Olga is very private about her background," Alexandra replied. "You will learn about her in good time after she has become confident that she can trust you. You will be surprised to learn about her. She has lived a life of complications and on the edge of danger for most of her early years."

As Nadia met other *agency* women living in the house, she was struck by the wide variety of types of women that had entered Olga's system. However, essentially all had been recruited through the mail-order-bride program. They had all come from poverty in search of a better life and were willing to do anything and take big chances to get it.

After a few days of getting settled in, Olga summoned Nadia to a meeting in the drawing room, where she laid out the first phase of the plan for her. Nadia was to embark on a crash course to improve her English language skills. She needed to learn to talk like an educated woman. She needed the facility to converse with affluent people about cultural, political, and financial matters. She also needed to learn about etiquette and proper conduct in social situations.

Nadia was a quick study and embraced the self-improvement program with enthusiasm. As Nadia progressed quickly in her education, Olga decided it was time to move her into a role with more client visibility. She promoted Nadia to become part of the team that interfaced with clients to plan the events and organize the activities necessary to run them successfully.

This required another phase of Nadia's development. Alexandra arranged for regular visits to a hair and nail salon and took her shopping for more attractive clothes. A whole new world opened up for Nadia, and she loved it.

All along she wondered why Olga had taken such a high level of interest in her. Nadia was not your typical Russian beauty. She was not a tall, classic, blue-eyed blonde like Alexandra and many of the others at *the agency*. In her late twenties, she was also a little older than most of them. What did Olga mean that she was "stealth-like," and why was that important to her?

Because she had suffered affection deprivation in the orphanage as an infant, as a child, and as a youth growing up, Nadia struggled to understand matters of an emotional nature. She had never experienced friendship or romance and was a stranger to love.

While she had a soft, shy manner, what distinguished her most was that she was mentally gifted, to a very high level. Her extraordinary intelligence was not easily discerned because of her reserved demeanor and the long hard life that she had as a youth. Also, the early struggle in her life, just to survive, had given her an inner strength that was not immediately obvious.

Olga saw the high potential in her. What Olga liked was the potent combination of Nadia's approachable, natural beauty and her recondite high intelligence.

Thanks to the diligence of her mail-order-bride affiliate, she had learned that when Nadia was in college, one of her professors, impressed with the girl's intellectual potential, suggested that she take the Mensa exam. The professor had explained to her that the Mensa exam was designed to evaluate the intelligence of genius-level individuals. She did it for the fun of it and scored "off the charts"—in the professor's estimation—not knowing the significance of what she had done. But Olga knew the Mensa test revealed one's raw intelligence, independent of language skill or knowledge. Olga was intrigued and knew she had to recruit this young woman into her enterprise.

It finally came to a point when it was time to test her in a live, field situation. Could Nadia follow the script? Could she carry out the mission without letting her sympathy for another person get in the way?

This first test would be away from the home base target area of West LA. Olga selected the coastal town of Newport Beach, just sixty miles south of Los Angeles. No one would recognize her there, and if the test failed, there would be no loss.

So it was that Olga orchestrated the encounter at Pelican Hill.

# CHAPTER 5

# FIRST SERIOUS MISSION

A YEAR AFTER JOINING OLGA'S ORGANIZATION, Nadia had successfully completed a number of small training exercises. She had also moved along quickly in her "studies" and development. Olga had promoted her in the *Beverly Hills Event Management Company* to a higher level of responsibility. Nadia was now ready to move up to her first high-level target.

Bernard and Veronica Haussmann were prominent philanthropists in the social scene on the city's west side. Bernard was the CEO of the Richman Company, a large private firm that manufactured and sold household appliances domestically and internationally. These days most of the manufacturing was offshore.

Bernard was a man of some distinction, with dark hair graying at the temples. At sixty-two, he had been married to Veronica since his late twenties. Bernard had met Veronica when he worked at the company as a young engineer. Her family owned the company, which helped his career path considerably. Nepotism aside, he had become a very good CEO and leader for the company. He also was widely respected in his industry and the LA community.

Veronica had grown up with wealth. She had attended a private boarding school in the east and graduated from an Ivy League university. She traveled easily in the higher circles of society. Bernard was a handsome young engineer when they met, and a romance quickly ensued. They were married a few years after graduating from college.

Bernard came from a blue-collar family and worked his way through college. He was a conscientious student who hit the books religiously and earned good grades. As a young man he had distinguished himself in the Richman Company. Even without his relationship with Veronica's family, he probably would have progressed through the company's ranks. He had reached the executive vice president level when Veronica's father, who had been running the company for decades, decided to retire. Bernard was the logical successor and was promptly appointed to become the company's new CEO. That was years ago now, and Bernard had done a superb job of building the company over the years that followed.

As a good and loyal husband, Bernard seemed like an unlikely target. Furthermore, there had never been even the slightest rumor of an affair on his part. However, Olga had him in her sights and thought she had an effective "weapon" to get to him. It was Nadia.

Bernard was in good shape for his age and was still a virile man. Veronica's once beautiful face showed the telltale ravages of age, and she had become a little overweight. In public there was an absence of evidence of affection between them—no touching, never a small kiss or an admiring gesture of any kind. Veronica seemed always busy with her personal interests and philanthropic endeavors. She seldom mentioned Bernard in her conversations and had grown inattentive to him. She took him for granted. He had his business, played golf with his buddies, and had many interests. Veronica was comforted by the fact that they had affluence, and she was very secure in their relationship.

Olga suspected that beneath his strong outward countenance, Bernard was growing unhappy in his marriage. His work and position in the community remained vitally important to him. And then there was the fact that Veronica's family still owned a controlling interest in the company he managed. His identity was all wrapped up in being CEO of the Richman Company. He was pretty much trapped in the relationship. But that was okay with him because he had status in the community, the business was going very well, and he had many good male friends.

When Bernard traveled on business trips, Veronica was always too busy to go with him. She was constantly busy with her charity board activities, her ladies' bridge club, and with extended travel with her lady friends. Consequently, Bernard often found that he was home alone in the evening having dinner by himself. The companionship that he once shared with Veronica had faded, and he often was lonely.

*Kirke, the enchantress/sex goddess from Homer's Odyssey.*

Olga was ready to give Nadia her first assignment, and Bernard Haussmann was the target. One day, she called Nadia into the drawing room at the Malibu house for an extensive mission briefing to prepare her for the project.

Olga began with an orientation that laid out her philosophy about men and about women's relationship to them. She described the "male animal" as a very primal human being. She continued that Mother Nature had made them that way in order to perpetuate the species. Men were built to be the pursuers in seeking procreation. It was simply the way of the world.

"Men are such simple creatures," she opined to Nadia, a note of contempt in her voice. "It is women that choose the best-of-breed to mate with, not men. It produces a better genetic offspring that way. For men, mating is an uncontrolled, primal instinctive act. For women, it is a thoughtful, strategic selection process. Therein lays the *power of womankind*. In the game of life, a man is no match for a woman who understands that principle and uses her assets and skills wisely.

"Nature has endowed men with larger size, physical strength, and the proactive, aggressive disposition to be the 'hunters' and the providers in a relationship or family unit," Olga went on. "They are the 'workhorses' in the social order. Men think of themselves as the patriarch of a family unit and to be the 'chief executives' in relationships. It is good for us women to let them believe that illusion … but, of course, it is not true."

Nadia wondered, *Where is Olga going with this, and why is it relevant?*

Olga continued. "Females, on the other hand, are the *provocateurs*. Their role is to make themselves so desirable that dominant males are compulsively drawn to them. Nature has constructed this scheme so that males have little control over their behavior when confronted by an attractive female. In the presence of a sexy female, men lose all ability to think or act in a rational way. This is an enormous source of power for women that know how to use it.

"While on the surface it may seem that males are the predators that seek out and select females, in fact, it is the other way around. Females select and target the best of the male species.

"Men tend to be obvious, while females are more subtle and manipulate events to suit their purpose. Men are endowed with brawn and domineering personalities. Women, with their smaller, more delicate stature, are endowed with *finesse* … a much more powerful attribute.

"Men are completely unsuspecting in this process, largely because they do not think that way and regard—incorrectly—women to be inferior. They start with a presumption that they are in charge of matters. A dominant male would never suspect that he was being manipulated like a marionette on a woman's stage.

"Nadia, when you understand this, you will be able to beat men at their own game, every time. I will help you to do it, and it will make you into an extremely potent and successful lady."

*Illustration is by Picasso (1934)
for Lysistrada (411 B.C.),
the Greek comedy where women
ban together, denying men sexual
pleasures until they ended the war
between Athens and Sparta.*

Nadia was amazed to hear Olga talk this way. Was it wisdom, or did she just have a bad attitude about men? Nadia had never felt power in a relationship with a man. She had always been dependent on them. Nadia's selection of men had been limited to what was essential for her survival. Although her experience with men had been largely dismal, she was reluctant to believe that Olga's basic characterization applied to all men. Alexandra had told her a little bit about Olga's earlier life, many years ago, as a CIA agent in Eastern Europe when she had to use her feminine wiles to conduct intelligence missions. Perhaps that had contributed to her critical biases toward men.

Nadia thought about the enormous contrast between Olga and Alexandra. Olga seemed to have a low opinion of men and perhaps didn't like them very much. But Alexandra loved them, found them interesting … and was excited to engage them in intimate relationships. *How different these two ladies are!* she thought.

Olga renewed her lecture. "It is critical for the women assigned to my projects that they don't let their emotions, personal ethics, or sympathy get in the way of the mission. While those are important considerations, one must remain focused and not become overly philosophical about such matters. As an *agent* you will need to be able to move with cunning and resolve … and have the feline skills to manipulate the target successfully. An essential ingredient in the acquisition of your power is the development of a trusting relationship between you and the target. An *agent* needs to develop the complete trust of a targeted male if she is to be effective with him.

"I have a plan for your first assignment. Are you ready?" Olga asked.

"Yes! I would like to get started," Nadia responded enthusiastically.

Olga then proceeded to outline the plan for the Bernard Haussmann mission.

As a couple the Haussmanns were big supporters of the arts in Los Angeles, and this summer they were hosting a gala at their home in Bel Air for the LA Philharmonic Society. *The Beverly Hills Event Management Company* had been engaged to run the event for them, and Nadia was assigned to be the event coordinator.

A planning meeting was scheduled at the Haussmanns' home to organize activities for the gala event. Veronica normally was an active participant in those meetings, but she happened to be on a cruise with her sister at the time of the initial meeting. The timing was not entirely accidental, since Olga was privy to the Haussmanns' general affairs, including their travel schedules.

Olga, Nadia, and two other staff members attended the meeting along with Bernard and the two LA Philharmonic co-chairs of the event. The meeting was very businesslike and lasted about two hours late one afternoon.

At its conclusion, Nadia asked, "Bernard, would you mind taking me on a tour of the property? Olga and the others have been here many times before and know it well, but I have not. It would be helpful for my planning efforts to see the entire layout of the estate."

"I would be delighted," he responded.

And so the others left, and Bernard guided Nadia on a leisurely tour of the house and grounds of his magnificent estate.

That day Nadia was wearing a simple black silk dress. While businesslike, it hugged her curvaceous body like a second skin. Bernard could not help notice that no panty line showed under the fragile silk fabric.

The Haussmann estate was an impressive property, and Nadia took every opportunity to compliment Bernard on it. She showed interest in him personally, asking about his company, about his art collection, and other things that Olga had told her about. She was following the script to make him feel good about her.

The Haussmann estate was an ideal site for the LA Philharmonic summer party. It was a spacious home in a classic Spanish style with expansive, manicured lawns and gardens that were framed by hedges sculptured in an artistic way. Topiary and sumptuous flower gardens were alive with a riot of color. There were a number of impressive terraces that overlooked the grounds of the property. Nadia and Bernard continued to talk as they toured the site.

The tour took about an hour and finished at dusk.

"Would you care to join me for a glass of wine?" Bernard asked.

Nadia, of course, accepted the invitation. As they sat on the terrace Bernard opened a bottle of Ornellaia, from the Bolgheri region of Italy, and offered her a long-stemmed glass half-filled with the fragrant red wine. Nadia complimented him on his choice.

"I love the Super Tuscans. They are wonderful blends that are to Italy what the Bordeaux are to France. Actually, I believe they are better."

Bernard was impressed. "You are knowledgeable about wines?"

"Yes, but on my income, I cannot afford to buy fine wines. It's a pleasure to actually have an opportunity to enjoy one. Two thousand and one was a very good vintage year."

Actually, a thorough orientation in fine wines was part of Nadia's education program, since it is an area of expertise important in dealing with high net worth clients.

Bernard was curious about Nadia. "You have an accent. It sounds like eastern European or Russian. If you don't mind my asking, where are you from ... and what brought you to America?"

Olga had prepared Nadia for this inevitable query and needed to be somewhat evasive. It would be unwise for Bernard to know about the mail-order-bride matter or the fact that she had been married to an Encino plumbing contractor. So the storyline that she shared with Bernard was different.

"I was born in Russia, grew up there, and came to America as a graduate student. I ran out of money and had to drop out of school. I was fortunate to get a job with Olga's event management company."

As they sat there talking and enjoying the wine, Bernard found Nadia increasingly interesting. She offered stimulating conversation on a wide range of topics. She was amazingly well informed on global issues, even though she was more than thirty years his junior. In the warm light of the setting sun, he thought how beautiful she looked. It was a welcome pleasure for him to spend some time with such an attractive young woman.

It had come time for Nadia to head back to the Malibu house. Announcing that she was leaving, she reached across the table and touched Bernard's arm in appreciation for the tour and glass of wine. The contact with her warm hand sent a surge of unexpected excitement through his body. He thought, *How could a simple touch do so much to arouse me?*

That night, as he dined alone as usual, thoughts of Nadia dominated his mind: her beautiful young body, the absence of a panty line, the pleasant conversation, her relaxed smile ... and those amazing deep blue eyes that had looked at him across the table. It was all that he could think about. Nadia had taken the first step in *possessing* him.

The next morning, Nadia received a call from Bernard. He said that there were a few items that he wanted to go over with her about the event plan. She readily agreed to meet him for lunch.

They met at a restaurant on the beach in Malibu, near where she lived at Olga's big house. Bernard made up some items to discuss with her, but it was obvious to Nadia that he simply wanted more contact with her. At this point he had no idea where he wanted to take things with her. He even felt a little uncomfortable that being seen with her in a public place might raise suspicions, if they were noticed alone together. He rationalized that the business aspect justified their meeting together.

The lunch meeting did nothing to subdue his attraction to her. She continued to engage him in thoughtful conversation, showed him respect and admiration, and led him to believe that she considered him a handsome man. As he looked at her across the table he was again taken by how beautiful she was. Today she was simply wearing black slacks that fit tightly over her slender hips and a white cotton blouse that revealed the sensual contour of her bust line. She wore no jewelry. It was driving him crazy!

*I wish I were twenty years younger and single,* he thought. *She seems attracted to me, even at my age. If only I could extend our relationship beyond a business context. I think she would be receptive.* But, as he thought about Veronica and his social standing in the community, he knew it would be a disastrous adventure to "cross the line" into a relationship with this woman.

Nadia was acutely tuned into his dilemma. She needed to pull him back into her clutches and away from his reluctance.

"You seem pensive today," she observed. "Is something on your mind?"

"No, I was just enjoying the moment, and perhaps my mind drifted away. Sorry."

Nadia reached across the table knowingly and grasped his hand with a little squeeze. This was the same touch that had excited him on the evening at his home. For the moment, his apprehension melted away as he returned to the connection with her.

The setting for their lunch was divine. Bernard had arranged for a nice table outside under a trellis through which the sun's warm rays streamed. The restaurant was nestled on the beach, and Nadia could gaze across the sand to the ocean's waves breaking along the shore. They enjoyed almost two hours together, talking and occasionally sharing a little laugh about something amusing. Bernard was developing a strong attraction to her and a compelling desire to become more than friends with this extraordinary creature.

Over the next two weeks they met there a number of times. Each rendezvous became more intimate, in a casual sort of way. This time he greeted her with a little hug and a kiss on the forehead. He wanted to do more, but they were in a public place.

After their many rendezvous, Nadia took the initiative. "Our meetings over lunch are wonderful, but I would like more time with you and not just in a public place. Is there any chance that we could get away together some time in a more private place?"

For Bernard, the moment had come—the moment he wanted so much, but the moment he intensely feared. Desire overcame his apprehension, and he said, "I have a business trip to San Francisco on Thursday and Friday two weeks from now. There is a wonderful small hotel, called the Post Ranch Inn, in the Big Sur area. Would you meet me there for the weekend?"

As soon as he said it, he panicked. *What have I done? I barely know this woman, and I can't do this to Veronica. If I'm discovered in an affair, with my social standing in the community, it would ruin me!*

Before he could retract the invitation, she accepted, saying that she was flattered that a man of his stature would want to spend a weekend with her. She empathized with him in that their weekend would need to be very discreet. Nadia indicated that she would travel separately to rendezvous with him at the hotel. He would tell his office and Veronica that his meeting schedule had been extended two more days.

In the days that followed, Bernard was both exhilarated and fearful. He agonized over what he was doing. He had been a faithful husband for over thirty years, and the sanctity of his exclusive relationship was about to be broken. Even if Veronica never learned of the breach, some of the intimacy in their long relationship would be lost. This was not a small price to pay for an indiscretion.

He pondered if he could trust Nadia. Sure, the romance was long gone out of the relationship with Veronica, and the love that they once shared had faded, but they had a good life together and trusted each other. He might be flushing all that down the toilet. Another big fear was that, if the whole thing went public and blew up on him, Veronica's family, having control of the Richman Company, would surely fire him. This had the makings of a disaster.

There was simply too much to risk.

He reached for the phone and called Nadia to tell her that he had reconsidered and must back out of the Post Ranch Inn rendezvous. Olga had prepared Nadia for this moment. She knew that it would come. Once Bernard thought about the possible repercussions, he would get cold feet and back out. Nadia needed to be prepared to handle his reluctance.

As Bernard explained his decision, to cancel their getaway, he could sense her disappointment at the news. "I understand," she said. "I know this puts you in a potentially compromising situation." On the other end of the line, he heard her cry a little.

"My luck has not been good with men; they have used me for the most part," Nadia went on tearfully. "I believed that you were different, a classy guy that respects women."

She paused and said with a sigh, "I have never been to a nice place like the Post Ranch Inn. I was so thrilled with the prospect of a weekend there and the opportunity to enjoy some private time with you.

"Bernard, you can completely trust me. I will tell no one about our weekend."

She had hit his soft spot. It was too much for him, and Bernard relented. He agreed to go ahead with the plan. Although he felt some anxiety about it, he was confident that she could keep it a secret.

It was late spring, and there was a mild chill in the air at Big Sur. The rugged coastline was fabulously beautiful from the cliffs, high

above the sea, where the Post Ranch Inn is located. One could look out at the Pacific Ocean, and, from that height, it looked like it stretched out forever. The small, private Post Ranch Inn was the perfect romantic getaway. For Nadia, this was a long way from the orphanage at Bryansk, Russia, where she had grown up.

Also, in spite of the mission that she was on, it was an opportunity to spend some time with a man of sophistication—a man that had sincere affection for her. This would be the first time for her to experience such an encounter.

Bernard was already there when she arrived late on that Friday afternoon. She greeted him with a big hug that eased the tensions in the air. There was a veranda off their room where they sat and enjoyed a glass of wine to watch the sun go down. It was an idyllic setting, and, sensing the inner conflict that Bernard was continuing to experience, Nadia reached over and took his hand. It was as if to say, "It's okay."

They did not go to the restaurant for dinner that night. Instead they ordered a few light items from room service. They continued to talk, enjoying the fabulous scene of nature before them.

They lay side by side in the bed and exchanged small talk. Bernard was on his back and Nadia was on her side facing him. Nadia cuddled up to him. Her warm, soft body felt *really good* to him. She ran her hand across his chest and down his stomach, but went no farther. He was aroused.

Olga's schooling had prepared Nadia for the variety of such encounters that she would face with men. Some would be aggressive and confident; some would be uncomfortable, reluctant, and passive. Clearly, Bernard fell into the latter category. However, Olga and Alexandria had tutored Nadia on how to handle these sensitive situations. With Bernard, she needed to take it slow and make him feel at ease.

He turned on his side, facing her. She rolled over, turning her back to him, and snuggled close. He embraced her, caressing her neck and ear. Nadia pressed her derriere into his body and his arousal elevated. Nadia thought, *There is nothing wrong with this man's biology. This is going to be easier than I thought.* As their sexual engagement progressed, Bernard moved his hand tentatively across her body. He could sense her arousal. She moaned in pleasure. The feedback bolstered his confidence. Near the end of it, she was on top of him. Except for a few small casual kisses they really hadn't kissed romantically. As they reached a peak of excitement, she leaned over and kissed him passionately.

When Bernard awakened the next morning, he saw Nadia standing nude, looking out to the sea. She was silhouetted against the panorama beyond the large window in the room. There she was, taking in the great beauty of the rugged Pacific coastline, standing there in the pure form that nature had created her ... obviously engaged in thoughtful reflection on the moment. His eye followed the contours of her sensuous body: the perfect shape of her bosom; her high slim derriere and flat tummy; her shapely legs. *What a marvelous creature*, he thought.

Bernard felt that a whole new dimension of his life had opened up. He had been living a life that was decidedly routine, driven by the momentum of daily activities mostly organized for him. It lacked adventure, spontaneity, and passion. This new woman lifted his spirits. He felt a surge of energy and vitality about his life … but all this with the backdrop of fear that he had entered the "danger zone."

Nadia clearly had pursued Bernard for a purpose that was not romantic in nature. However, after several weeks, she was beginning to know and appreciate him on a personal basis. Although he was the target for her mission, she did have some feelings for him.

Bernard was a decent, caring human being and had entered the affair with trepidations. He knew that he was violating the intimate trust relationship with Veronica, a trust that had been earned over the course of a thirty-year relationship. Nadia could sense that what he was doing troubled him … yet he could not help himself.

The pleasure that he experienced with Nadia simply overwhelmed all consideration of reason or moral principle. The temptation to enjoy passion and sexuality again was too great for him to resist.

Nadia also thought about their affair with some mixed emotions. The sexual act was different for her, in part, because of his age. This was not an out-of-control "young stallion." Bernard was more affectionate, less primal, than other men that she had been with. He was content to take it slow, to touch her caringly… and she knew that he liked her.

Perhaps, because of that, she did not find the experience as unpleasant as she might have anticipated. It was just different. It was a different way to experience the sensuality between her and a man.

Because she had some affection for him, she struggled with the lack of sincerity in what she was doing. Yet, she could feel good about the fact that she gave him a pleasure that was absent in his life.

Olga had warned her that she would face these emotional conflicts in the missions that she pursued. It was part of the complexities that went along with her "profession," and she needed to get comfortable with it.

Bernard returned from the trip and re-entered his "real world." Life was back to normal ... or was it? He would never be the same after Nadia had touched him.

The Richman Company was in the process of making a big acquisition, and, as the CEO, he was immersed in the deal. But all he could think about was Nadia. With his busy schedule and the threat of discovery, arranging a liaison was problematic. In the weeks that followed he would meet her at the Malibu restaurant for lunch or a late afternoon cocktail. But he was obsessed and wanted all of her. He dreamed nightly of the fantastic sex that they had in Big Sur. He had never experienced anything like it.

Bernard had to return to San Francisco to meet with the investment bankers on his acquisition deal and asked Nadia if she could get away for two days during the week. Nadia said that Olga had promised her some time off, but that it was a busy season. Since Olga was part of the plan, Nadia was able to get back to Bernard with the good news. She would meet him there.

While Bernard was tied up during the day, they were able to enjoy the city together in the evenings ... and, of course, to "sleep" together— an old-fashioned euphemism that made Bernard feel slightly less guilty about cheating on his wife. Bernard arranged for Nadia to go shopping during the day while he was in meetings and to have spa treatments at the hotel. Bernard was getting in deeper and falling for Nadia. Not only was she a gorgeous woman, she was totally engaging, and she was very attracted to him (or so he thought).

He wanted to see her more regularly back in LA, but the problem persisted: how to do it? Bernard had been careful not to have his name on anything that might trace him back to Nadia or any illicit activity. At the Post Ranch Inn he had paid in cash and put the room under Nadia's name. There was no record of him being there. Likewise he had paid cash at the restaurant, so his credit card wouldn't reflect the charge.

He wanted to get her out of the Malibu house, so she would be free to meet him whenever he wanted. Olga controlled the women that worked for her *agency* with a tight grip. She monitored all of their comings and goings, their bank accounts, and external relationships.

In the morning, before their return from San Francisco, Bernard told Nadia that he wanted to step up their relationship.

"I want you out of Olga's house and business, so I can see you whenever I want," he said assertively. "I am willing to financially support you to make this possible. We can rent a nice apartment in West LA, and I will provide you a generous allowance to live on. Of course, my name cannot be on the apartment lease, but I will provide you the money to rent it."

"That would be wonderful." Nadia said. "I am falling for you and have hoped that we could spend more private time together. Leaving Olga's employment, the house, and her support is a frightening thing for me. If you drop me, Olga will not take me back. She will be angry if I leave," she added in a convincingly apprehensive tone.

"I will not leave you," Bernard assured her.

"But you intend to stay married to Veronica, yes?" Nadia said in a concerned voice.

"Yes, at least for now. I cannot easily get out of my marriage, even though I am not happy in it. Perhaps at some point—"

"Bernard!" Nadia interrupted. "I want to be with you, but you will need to provide me with some significant security, if I am to gamble on our relationship."

"What would you need?"

"Perhaps we could buy a condo rather than rent an apartment, and you could put some cash in my account. I have no savings to get by on if you leave me."

Bernard, concerned that Veronica might find out, replied, "My name could not be on the title. It's too big a risk for me. You have no credit history, so a mortgage is out of the question. It would have to be a cash purchase. I can get you some regular money, but any big money transfer to you would be impossible since it would be traceable back to me."

"I understand, but there must be a way. You are a clever businessman. Do you have any ideas?"

An idea occurred to Bernard.

"There might be a way. My company will be closing on a good-sized acquisition soon. It is commonplace for companies to pay finder's fees to individuals and firms that introduce opportunities of this kind to buyers. You could set up a bank account with a company name that sounds like a financial or consulting firm. I could send you a letter contract on the Richman Company letterhead specifying a finder's fee for the deal. When it closes, that fee would go directly to the account on which you are the sole signer."

"That is brilliant!" Nadia enthused. "I will set up the account and get you the necessary information on it."

Bernard was pleased with the brilliance of the scheme. The funds transfer would not come out of his joint account with Veronica and therefore not raise any suspicion. To the company it would be an ordinary cost of the transaction. Nadia set up an account in the name of the Bingham Financial Corporation, the supposed intermediary in the acquisition.

Nadia went out looking for a condo the next day and found one in the Westwood area. It was on the twelfth floor of a very nice building. She described it to Bernard and said the owner was desperate to sell. They could time the escrow to close just after the acquisition by the Richman Company. It would take about two million dollars to make the purchase. She would need another $250,000 to buy furniture and have the condo painted and $50,000 to provide her some independent spending money. So the finder's fee would need to be 2.3 million dollars, an amount that was reasonable considering the size of the acquisition that the Richman Company was making.

This scheme would take no money out of his pocket and would look completely legitimate. The beauty of this scheme was that there would be no traceability of a payment from him to Nadia. Deal costs like this were common, and he had signed off on them before. So the plot continued.

At one of their rendezvous, Bernard asked if he could see the condo. Nadia said that she would let him do a drive-by to show him where it was, but she wanted their first night there to be special. She wanted to get the furniture in and the place painted in preparation for the treat that she had in store for him. It would be a night to remember!

Bernard could hardly wait. The acquisition was progressing on schedule. He had turned over the finder's fee letter contract to his CFO to incorporate the payment into the transaction costs when the deal closed. It would be automatic. This was along with the other payments to legal counsel, the audit firm, investment banks, and others. Along with the finder's fee contract, he provided the wire transfer instructions to the account of Bingham Financial Corp., the firm that had connected Bernard to the acquisition target.

It became part of the routine of the closing, and the funds showed up the next day in Nadia's account. She had told Bernard that everything was lined up. The condo purchase would close the day after the acquisition and the painters and movers were ready to go. They could enjoy their first night there in a week.

It was a very long week for Bernard as his anticipation grew. He dreamed of the sexual pleasure that lay ahead and the new life this arrangement offered them. At last the time had come. Nadia told him to arrive at the condo at 6:00 pm the next day. The building security officer would be advised to let him in.

When he arrived that day he was greeted at the entrance by the security guard. He told him that he was there to visit Nadia. The guard looked at him strangely and said, "There is no one here by that name."

"Your list must not be up to date," said Bernard, a bit flustered. "She purchased Unit 1285 a week ago."

"I'm sorry, sir, but no units have been sold in this building for a year," the guard assured him.

There was a sinking feeling in Bernard's stomach. Something was wrong ... very wrong.

He went back to his car and called Olga's house, hoping to find Nadia there. Alexandra, Nadia's roommate, answered the call. He asked for Nadia. Alexandra told him that Nadia had suddenly packed her bags and returned to Russia. He asked for Olga, who was available and took his call. Not wanting his inquiry to seem of a personal nature, he said that Alexandra had reported to him that Nadia had left the country unexpectedly.

"Is that true?" Bernard demanded angrily. "And how in the hell is your firm going to manage the LA Philharmonic charity event with your coordinator gone?"

"I was as surprised as you, Mr. Haussmann," Olga replied evenly. "I already have a competent replacement to step in as our project coordinator. Do not worry. Everything for the charity event will go smoothly."

Of course he was not concerned about the charity event; he really wanted to find Nadia.

"Do you know where Nadia can be reached?"

"No, she simply left a note thanking me for everything ... for turning her life around. But she was returning to Russia. She left no forwarding address or contact information."

Bernard's next call was to the bank where the wire transfer had been made. From the acquisition transaction documents, he had the account number and the wire transfer instructions. He told the bank manager that he was "just following up to make sure the funds had arrived." The bank manager confirmed that the funds had arrived, but added that the account had been closed.

This was a disaster. But he was in a tough position; he could not tell anyone about it. To do so would be to admit that he had engaged in a fraudulent scheme to misappropriate company funds.

So he was condemned to live with the secret for the rest of his life.

But he would also live with the vivid memory of his romantic adventure with Nadia. The raven-haired beauty had touched him, and he would never be the same again.

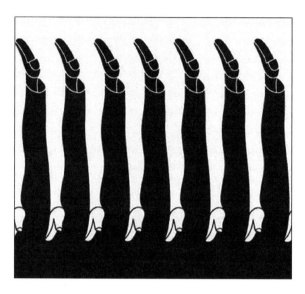

*"Legs of Two Different Genders", Shigeo Fukuda*

# CHAPTER 6

# OLGA AND
# *THE AGENCY*

AFTER THE HAUSSMANN AFFAIR, NADIA WAS laying low for a few days at the San Ysidro Ranch, a small hotel in Montecito, near Santa Barbara, California. Olga had put her up there, and she loved it. Nadia was intrigued by its storied history. Jack and Jackie Kennedy had honeymooned there. Winston Churchill had written his memoirs there.

The Ranch is nestled in the foothills above the small exclusive town of Montecito and is a rich part of California history. It is canopied by ancient oak and eucalyptus trees and has a small creek that runs through the property. From the site, one has a panoramic view of the blue Pacific Ocean in the distance. The Ranch was originally a way station for the Franciscan monks dating back to 1769 and was converted to a guest ranch over a century ago, in 1893.

It is a private, unconventional, boutique hotel in that it consists of only forty-one guest accommodations located in historic cottages scattered around the site. For a long time it has been a favorite retreat for celebrities from the film industry in Los Angeles.

On that morning, Nadia had taken a long walk down the hill from the San Ysidro Ranch through the residential area below. It was an older part of Montecito, and the street was bordered by stately homes with very tall hedges providing the homes with a lot of privacy. She wondered about the people that lived there.

*Nadia's room at "the Ranch"*

As she strolled along, Nadia thought back to the mission that she had just completed. In most encounters between a man and a woman, the man is the seducer. It was interesting that, in her case, the roles were reversed. In the case of Haussmann, she found the seduction of the male species to be very easy.

She reflected on the affair with Bernard more deeply. It was not the money that she had extracted from him that she regretted; it was what she had destroyed in his life. Although Veronica would, most likely, never know what happened at the Post Ranch Inn, Bernard would *always* know. For him, something would have been lost. There was an intangible cost to the affair. On the other hand, he had been awakened to a dimension of life that he might never have known. Was it worth it? She knew that was a question that would haunt him for years.

Nadia had never been fortunate enough to have a deep, caring love relationship with a man. However, she had often thought about the attributes that she would hope to have in a relationship ... about the basic principles of romance, intimacy, and trust.

In her life she had little exposure to suitable men. Russian men were very chauvinistic and had a low regard for women. Others that she had met were not her intellectual peers and seemed to have only primal motives with their women.

With the right man, she would hope to be able to share her deepest fears, aspirations, and views about life. Real intimacy could only be achieved through trust and continuing exclusivity … yet she wondered whether love was anywhere in her future. She had always led a "lone wolf" type of life.

It was not clear to her that a romantic relationship was in the cards for her with any man. Olga appeared to have a good life without a male companion. Nadia, herself, had no maternal instincts. She struggled to understand where men might fit—or might not—into her future. To Nadia, these were the complications of life and the consequences of her new "professional" endeavors.

At some point, Nadia's morning walk was over. She walked up to the pool area of the hotel, where she changed into a swimsuit and resumed her exercise, swimming laps in the pool.

The swimming pool area at the San Ysidro Ranch is located at the top of the property, well above the cottages and other facilities. It has a commanding view across Montecito to the ocean, but on a late afternoon everyone disappears from the pool area. Nadia remained there alone, soaking up the last rays of the late summer sun.

Time flew by for Nadia, and now Olga was coming to visit her. She looked forward to it with anticipation. Nadia was tired of all the secrecy that surrounded Olga. If she was going to continue to work in Olga's enterprise, she wanted to know more about her and her background and *the agency*.

Olga had made the drive up the coast and joined her. She walked up the steep path to meet Nadia and was panting a little because of the climb.

Olga sat in a chair at poolside next to Nadia, who was reclining in a chaise longue. Olga had not had the opportunity to see Nadia in a bathing suit before. She was wearing large dark sunglasses and a red bikini. Beads of water still glistened on her smooth skin, a little pink from the afternoon sun. As Olga examined Nadia's flawless young body, she thought, *This is a lethal weapon, if ever I saw one!*

"Nadia, you did a terrific job on the Haussmann assignment! I have put $50,000 in a local checking account for your use and the rest of your share, $1.1 million, in an offshore Swiss bank account. The information on your offshore account and the local account are all in the passbooks that have been placed on the table in your room.

"So, my dear, how does it feel to be a millionaire?"

Nadia looked over at Olga. She took off her sunglasses and spoke in a contented tone. "Olga, all my life I have struggled just to survive. To have some financial security is a wonderful feeling. Would you like a glass of wine?"

Olga looked at the ice bucket next to Nadia and noticed a bottle of Corton Charlemagne. "I see you're developing a taste for the finer things in life. That's a very nice white Burgundy."

Nadia smiled. "I owe it all to you."

"You have been a fast learner and have already demonstrated a talent for our trade," Olga said.

"Thank you, but I want to know more about you," Nadia inquired with interest. "How did you get to where you are in life? And I would like to know more about *the agency*."

Olga was a very private person and seldom shared any information about her past. However, she was developing a fondness for Nadia. Perhaps she could see, in this young woman, a nostalgic glimpse of herself some thirty years earlier. Perhaps Nadia could become like the daughter she never had.

Nadia served her a glass of wine and Olga began to talk … and reminisce.

"I was born in Kiev, the largest city in the Ukraine. My parents, both university professors at the prestigious Taras Shevchenko National University, escaped the country and came to America when I was young. They had been persecuted, and at times jailed, for their opposition to the Soviet rule and their activist role in seeking freedoms in the

Ukraine. They knew of many other dissenters that had been tortured and killed by the secret police of the KGB."

"It was fortunate that they were able to get out," Nadia remarked. "What did you do in America?"

"In America I did very well in school and graduated from college with honors. After graduation, I was recruited into the CIA. My Russian language skills and understanding of technology had something to do with my appeal to them, I suppose. This was during America's Cold War with the Soviet Union, and the CIA needed staff that could speak the language with authenticity."

"I have heard that you were assigned to Europe," Nadia prompted her.

"You heard correctly. With the Cold War raging, I was quickly groomed for clandestine missions overseas. As a young woman I was very attractive, and the agency believed that my beauty would help me gain access to information that would have been difficult for a man to acquire. I served as a CIA operative to run many missions deep into the Soviet leadership, even into the secret service activities of the KGB."

"That sounds dangerous," Nadia said, beginning to understand why Olga was such a tough lady.

"It was dangerous work, but I hated the Soviets. My disdain was for the political leaders, not the Russian people, who were abused as much as were the people in the other nations of the USSR. During that period of my life, I virtually never lived in America although I served my country with devotion."

"On what kind of assignments were you deployed?" Nadia asked.

"With the escalation of the Cold War conflict, my duties became increasingly critical. Intelligence gathering and espionage were at a high point. These activities also became even more dangerous. It was not uncommon for one of my colleagues to get captured, tortured, and killed." Olga shook her head in sad reflection. "I knew all too well the penalty that would await me, if I was discovered.

"At times I had to put my personal feelings aside and do what needed to be done on my assignments," Olga admitted reluctantly. "After acquiring secret information, it would occasionally be necessary to eliminate the enemy source so as not to leave any trail of my spying operation. Often the Soviet official, from whom I obtained the information, would be one with which I had cavorted with and had come to know personally."

She paused, finding it difficult to continue. "While this made the task of killing more difficult, it was a necessary part of my mission. Leaving one behind could compromise the mission and, perhaps, even lead to the death of another fellow CIA operative. I always disliked the messiness of firearms, so my weapon of choice was a substance called ricin. It induced cardiac failure, but left no trace of toxicity. Thus, it always appeared that my 'target' had died of natural causes."

"I don't think I could do it," Nadia said with a shudder.

"In that line of work, you get hardened after a while," Olga replied. "We were on our own when working in deep cover. If any one of us were caught, the US government would disavow our existence.

"In my role there, I developed a reputation as somewhat of a wild party girl. I guess it was true. It provided some relief from the pressure of the job, but also helped me gain the attention of the Soviets that I was targeting. During those years I was often seen at hot spots in Prague, Vienna, Budapest, and other cities in Eastern Europe. At times I was in Russia itself. I tended to drink a lot and play hard, but always with the discipline of the mission behind it all."

"How could you get the government and military officers to give you secret information?" Nadia asked.

"When I was young ..." Olga sighed. "Because I was a very attractive woman, it was easy to get men in the Soviet leadership to pursue me. I could easily talk them into sharing information. I would simply appear to be impressed with their military expertise. I would acknowledge that they must be important, because they had access to vital secrets. They were only too willing to impress me by talking more. It helped that they believed I was a Soviet loyalist. They did not have any suspicions about my motives. Their agenda was to get me to 'bed down' with them. Once a man gets sex on his mind, you can make him do anything."

Olga had a low opinion of men and had never married. It had always been easy for her to manipulate men using her sexual prowess. She professed to think of them as weak and undisciplined when confronted with feminine sensuality. She liked to say, "A man cannot look at a woman's breasts and think at the same time."

Despite Olga's seemingly unflattering view of men, Nadia saw Olga as a sophisticated woman with keen insights into people. She could not believe that Olga's real views of men were as negative as she portrayed.

"Olga, have you ever been in love?" Nadia asked.

"In my profession, I moved around a lot, I assumed many fake identities, and it was difficult to develop real world relationships."

Olga paused for a moment, and then continued with a faraway look in her eye. "There was a young officer in the British Secret Intelligence Service, referred to as the MI6 unit. Internally we referred to it as 'Box 850,' its post office box number. The CIA collaborated extensively with this British agency during World War II and the Cold War. I met him in Prague. A liaison evolved between us. It was in that relationship that I was first moved to love a man. I knew only his first name: Philip. Over the course of my career I have known many men 'intimately,' but the circumstances of my trade caused me to maintain my distance emotionally. I could not get involved.

"Philip, however, touched my heart. He captured me romantically. He was not a cold operative like the other men I encountered. He was a sensitive person capable of deeply caring for a woman. He also cared for others and was particularly distraught over the Soviets' horrific treatment of political dissenters. On his own, he aided them in defecting to the west, providing them with falsified documents and currency, and connecting them to his underground sources. This was dangerous and eventually led to his undoing. This was the sentimental side of him that I admired but could not share myself. My romance with him was one of the rare moments that I allowed myself to care about someone during those years."

Olga took a deep breath and continued. "However, to help others, he would take risks. When the Prague Spring uprising collapsed and the Red Army crushed the effort in Czechoslovakia, he escalated his aid to the dissidents. The KGB internal security forces were very effective in identifying the ringleaders. Anyone that helped the resistance movement was singled out by the secret police and killed. Philip's complicity in the movement was uncovered, and he was made to disappear.

"After that, I realized it was too risky to let one's personal feelings get involved."

Nadia looked at Olga with admiration and respect—amazed at her and the life that she had lived. This was a woman of extraordinary aplomb. Olga had "walked on the wild side" and had experiences that no other woman could imagine. While she seemed to have a negative attitude about men, she knew the many complexities of the male species in a very sophisticated way. Much of her knowledge arose out of four decades of close encounters with them and relationships that Nadia could only imagine.

Olga's hair had turned gray prematurely, perhaps as a consequence of the adventuresome life that she had lived. However, even at her age she was still a very attractive woman. She had retained her good figure through the years, and, while her skin betrayed some signs of her advancing years and the hardship of her career, there was a youthful energy about her.

This was a woman that had lived a life of danger from her early twenties until her early retirement when she was in her forties. During her career with the CIA she had traveled in high circles on an international basis and had partied with ministers of state, top military officers, and industrial leaders of the Eastern bloc and Russia. She was an alpha female, a very tough lady … worldly beyond what most could imagine.

"What did you do when the Cold War ended?" asked Nadia.

"When the confrontation with the Soviets came to an end, I was pretty burned out. I decided to leave my government post and wanted to go somewhere very different … somewhere where it was warm and I could start a new life. That desire took me to Southern California."

"How did you get started in your business in California?" Nadia asked.

"I was forty-six when I came west. I took a job in a charity events management company. A year later, I decided to go off on my own. That's when I started the *Beverly Hills Event Management Company.* Every day I came in contact with a lot of very wealthy people. I was a little bored with the day-to-day activity of the business and decided to add a little 'spice' to my life by using the skills that I developed with my old employer to pull off a sting on a rich guy that I met here in town.

"At first, I did it purely for fun and the excitement of it," Olga went on, smiling at the memory. "I realized, though, that at my age, I was a little old for that sort of thing. So I enlisted a young Russian woman that I had met to perform the assignments for me. She was pretty desperate, and I was able to help her.

"I kept getting ideas and opportunities like that, and so it gradually evolved into quite an enterprise. I needed a steady supply of 'talent' and the young woman I helped initially, whose name is Kassandra, wanted to return to Russia. That's when I came up with the mail-order-bride scheme. Kassandra now runs the website, recruits young women, and conducts background diligence for me. Appropriately, the name Kassandra means 'a woman who entangles men' in Russian. Much of what appears accidental to you … may not be. As you will recall, you talked to Kassandra when you were in Bryansk."

Nadia nodded as Olga went on. "Over the years my enterprise developed into a going concern with several divisions. The mail-order-bride program became a true win-win as, through it, I was able to recruit wonderful young women for my business and also lift them out of poverty and despair."

"Certainly, that was my case," Nadia offered.

Olga smiled. "Indeed, my child. I bought the Malibu house to provide a safe living place for the young immigrant women who, generally, had little ability to care for themselves. It became a special home for the young recruits and some agents in from 'field assignments.' *The Beverly Hills Event Management Company* employed the recruits while they were undergoing the initial stages of their training and development. *The agency* became my prime enterprise. The very best of my recruits eventually matriculated into it and started calling themselves *agents.* There their skills would be developed, their beauty would be enhanced, and they would become trained in my methods of extracting large amounts of money from wealthy, unsuspecting men."

Nadia had learned that, at any particular time, there would be perhaps a dozen *agents* in the field somewhere around the globe. Furthermore, there was an "alumni association" of those that had moved on and retired from *the agency*; some had even gotten married. The alumni were mostly in high places in society, and most had become quite wealthy through their missions as Olga's *agents.*

Olga owned the office building in which the events management company operated, but only a small fraction of its employees were in *the agency.*

Nadia was curious. "I noticed in riding the elevator that some people were going down to the basement. They required a security card to access the basement floor. What is going on down there?"

"That is where our operations center is located." Olga said. "You would be amazed to know how much it takes to support agents in the field. Our missions are very lucrative, complex, and even dangerous at times. Everything must be researched, thought through in advance, and executed perfectly.

"Nadia, you have just begun to scratch the surface of the dimensions of my enterprise. I believe that you have the potential to have a great deal of success with us, if you wish. *The agency* is a tight knit group of extraordinary and talented young women who have been groomed and trained for highly potent, economically rewarding missions. We take advantage of their female power over men to accomplish our objectives. The women in my *agency* are better than any CIA agent that I have known. Their assignments are not clandestine or military in nature; they are purely commercial enterprises."

All of the women in her enterprise knew that Olga cared deeply about them and genuinely wanted them to have a better life. She was unselfish in that way, but extremely disciplined. There were strict rules of conduct in her agency. Character mattered to her—a strange principle for one engaged in an enterprise of a duplicitous nature. Illicit activity not related to *the agency's* mission was prohibited. Any violation would likely result in expulsion.

Olga had lifted Nadia out of poverty and a life of despair. Nadia was deeply appreciative, and there was a lot that she could learn from her. Nadia looked forward with anticipation to what might lie ahead.

The sun was now setting and it was growing late. They continued their visit over dinner at the wonderful Stonehouse Restaurant on the property.

At dinner Olga commented, "Nadia, you have done well on your first assignment. You have over a million dollars in your Swiss bank account. Have you thought about what you would like to do with the money?"

Nadia shrugged. "Considering where I came from, it is wonderful to have financial security. However, the money means nothing to me."

"What do you mean?"

"At times, reflecting on the terrible conditions that orphans must face, I have considered that I might like to do something to help them," Nadia said in a reflective tone.

"If you think more seriously about doing something, I would like to help you," Olga said. "If you choose to do something in Russia, you must be careful. The system is very corrupt, and you cannot simply give money to the orphanages. It will find its way into the pockets of the government officials."

"Your help would be wonderful, Olga, but for now, I am enjoying the adventure and challenge of our missions ... and look forward to the next one."

Nadia paused, and then, after a thoughtful moment, continued. "There is one thing. In Bryansk, there was a girl—"

"Sarah?" Olga responded.

Nadia touched her little garnet ring with a sigh of affection.

"Yes. I became close to her, and she helped me when I had nothing. She introduced me to your website, and it changed my life. I would like to do something for her."

Olga nodded. "Kassandra, my affiliate in Russia, knows her through her activity on our website. She can help."

"Sarah gave me this ring, and I would like to give her one in return. It need not be expensive; it would be an expression of my appreciation and friendship. Perhaps it should be somewhat like the one she gave to me. Also, I would like to give her some money to make her life a little easier."

"We can arrange that," Olga said warmly.

Nadia reached into her purse and took out a letter she had written one lonely evening. "I would like you to include this letter," she said, and read aloud:

*My dearest Sarah,*

*I want you to know that I am well and think of you often. As you predicted, my journey to America has brought me a better life. The ring that you gave me has been with me every day since my departure from Russia. It is a personal treasure and a part of you that goes with me wherever I go. Perhaps it has had a hand in my good fortune. I will forever be grateful to you.*

 *Although much time has passed, I wanted to reciprocate with a gift of a ring to you. This gift is a reflection of my appreciation for what you did for me. It does not have any mysterious powers, but just as your ring has been for me, it will be a constant reminder of our friendship.*
*Nadia*

"Nadia, what a wonderful gesture! We will take care of it for you," Olga promised.

Olga wanted to understand more about Nadia's motivations.

"Nadia, you have said that you do not do this for the economic gain. Why, then, do you do it?"

Because they had a business relationship of sharing the bounty of their missions, Nadia was anxious about telling Olga about her true motivations. She decided to answer the question truthfully anyway.

"From my earliest childhood, I have never had material things. To have my basic needs met is, in and of itself, a blessing. I do not need more.

"I have learned that I really enjoy being immersed in challenging situations. What really intrigues me is the contest between a woman of some skill and highly successful males—in particular those at the top of their species. In what we do, I can explore those relationships in a dynamic way. That is really a thrill for me. I enjoy testing myself in an active, competitive personal engagement with men ... the best of them.

"So, it is much more about *the game* between men and women, than about the reward. The prize is winning—besting men who themselves are at the top of the male order. Men and women enter the arena with different skills and assets. It is the contest between the genders that interests me. For me, it's all about *the game*."

Olga leaned forward. "You are truly a unique young woman,

Nadia. I look forward to watching you develop, and we are going to enjoy some interesting experiences together."

Olga would stay overnight and not return to LA until the next day. In the morning she planned to brief Nadia on what she had planned for her, and Nadia was anxious to hear about it.

# CHAPTER 7

# INVICTUS

NADIA AND OLGA MET THE NEXT morning for breakfast. Olga began to lay out her scheme for Nadia's next assignment.

"Your next mission involves higher stakes," she said. "In about six months' time, the America's Cup series will be held in San Francisco. The super rich from all over the world will be coming to the City by the Bay. You have no concept of the scale of this racing series. Each participant will spend over $100 million just to compete. They will come from all over the globe. There are entries from the United Arab Emirates, China, France, Italy, Korea, Sweden, Spain, and New Zealand. There will be more multi-billionaires assembled there than at any other place on the planet."

"The Haussmann assignment was not difficult at all. Are you planning a mission for me in San Francisco?" Nadia said anxiously.

"Yes! That's what I wanted to discuss with you. To pull off a mission in this environment will require a much higher level of skill and cunning. The 'extraction scheme' will need to be much more sophisticated than the one we completed with Bernard Haussmann. Furthermore, your beauty will not offer the same advantage, since these men are surrounded by beautiful women … and can have them whenever they want. For this mission, we will need to rely more on your intellect and other skills."

"This sounds exciting! What will we be targeting?"

"My objective is to come away with ten to fifty million dollars, but I do not know yet how we will do it," Olga said. "We will need to discover the opportunities as we get deeper into the mission. With a mission target this big, we need to think ahead about how you exit from the situation with no traceability back to you.

"One of *the agency* girls is returning to Russia. She has left her American passport, driver's license, and, most importantly, her Social Security number. She is close enough to your appearance that we can get by with the identity switch. Her name is Tatyana; that will be your name for the San Francisco mission. Tatyana is a blonde, however, so you will need to bleach your hair and cut it shorter."

"I can do that. It will be fun."

"Very good. I have arranged a job for you as a hostess at the venerable St. Francis Yacht Club. It is not the host club for the Cup, because Larry Ellison is not a member. Ellison, always a maverick, is a member of the smaller Golden Gate Yacht Club. His *BMW Oracle* racing team won the Cup last and will defend it for the USA. However, the St. Francis Yacht Club is a powerhouse in the city and is likely to be a highly active venue during the racing series. I have leased a small but very nice apartment for you overlooking the bay, near the yacht club."

Olga took a small bite of croissant and shot Nadia a challenging look. "Are you ready for this assignment?"

"Yes, I can make the move in a few days."

Olga was delighted. This promised to be one of her most lucrative missions, if it could be successfully completed.

"Excellent! You have a lot to learn that is very different from your training heretofore. You need to understand about the history of the Cup, about yacht racing … and importantly, you must know everything about the players—owners, sponsors, crew, skippers, and so forth. I have prepared a briefing package for you and a dossier on all of the key people.

"You may also want to dust off your non-English language skills, perhaps French and Italian, since those are three of the challenger teams," Olga added.

Nadia got settled in her new place in San Francisco and really liked it. For the first time she had a place of her own and some financial security. Her apartment was on the second story of an old Victorian house in the Pacific Heights area. From her window she could look out across San Francisco Bay. It was a very small unit, but she loved it. The yacht club was an easy walk from her apartment.

It was a wonderful city, but she was on a mission and needed to focus on the task ahead. Also, she needed to get used to her new name: "Tatyana." In her free time, she was busy studying the briefing materials provided to her by Olga. The package was deeply researched, and Nadia wondered, *Did Olga have a research staff to investigate all these people and put together all this information? The St. Francis Yacht Club is a very exclusive place. How did Olga get me a job there?*

Nadia increasingly regarded Olga as having mysterious powers.

As the weeks went by, Nadia had the opportunity to meet and get casually acquainted with many of San Francisco's elite and a growing number of people in the yachting community. As the time approached for the America's Cup competition, anticipation began to rise in the city. Big yachts started to arrive in the bay daily. Many had reciprocity relations with the St. Francis Yacht Club, so the activity there continued to increase.

Yesterday, Larry Ellison's new yacht, the 288-foot *Musashi*, arrived. He had sold his larger yacht, the 545-foot *Rising Sun*, to music and film billionaire David Geffen a couple of years earlier. Ellison had complained that his larger yacht was relegated to the industrial part of any harbor because of its size, and he always found those locations very unpleasant.

The America's Cup had come to San Francisco through a tortured path. The "Old Mug," as the trophy has been called, is the oldest international trophy in sports. It was first won in 1851 by the schooner *America* in a race against the best sailing yachts in England. The challenge race was organized by the Royal Yacht Squadron to demonstrate the superiority of Britain's sailing fleet. The competition was sailed around the Isle of Wight. It has been said that when the queen of England was told that the *America* had finished first, she asked: "Who was second?" The race committee chairman responded, "Madam, there is no second place."

America would defend the Cup against all challengers for 122 years, the longest winning streak in history in any sport, until Dennis Conner lost it in 1983 to the Australian challenger.

The perennially maverick Aussies had long said, "If we ever win it, we will take it off the pedestal at the New York Yacht Club (where it had been for over a century), put it in the street, and piss on it."

After that it had changed hands on many occasions: to the Kiwis (New Zealand) and most recently to Switzerland, when it was won by multi-billionaire Ernesto Bertarelli. Larry Ellison was determined to bring the Cup back to America, and his long effort resulted in a victory in Valencia, Spain, in 2010. Now he must defend it against challengers from all over the globe.

Under Cup rules, challengers must participate in a series of races against each other for the right to race against the defender. That series of races is called the Louis Vuitton Series. The winner goes on to compete in a match racing series against the defender (in this case, the USA team *BMW Oracle*) for the America's Cup.

The America's Cup event has been run about every four years. Historically, the type of sailing yachts that compete has changed from time to time. In this series, the contenders would sail 72-foot catamarans that are regulated under the AC72 rule, which is designed to assure that the yachts are fairly similar in performance characteristics. In this way the race committee seeks to assure that the cup race is a test of sailing skill, not boat making technology.

Since the San Francisco Bay can be quite windy, races in fast cata-marans provide a high degree of excitement.

Nadia, now known as Tatyana, had been carefully observing the arrivals of large yachts in San Francisco Bay. The latest arrival was *Invictus*, a 245-foot Feadship owned by Roberto Bartolini, the sponsor of the Italian entry in the America's Cup competition. In his early forties, Bartolini was young, very rich, arrogant, and used to getting his way in everything he did. He was handsome and had curly black hair that is so typically Italian. Bartolini had a reputation as a womanizer, yet always had many beautiful women around him.

Bartolini had inherited a huge media conglomerate in Europe that had been founded by his grandfather and built up by his father. Both were now deceased, his father dying from a gunshot wound inflicted by a jealous husband of a woman that he had seduced.

Bartolini arrived one day at the St. Francis Yacht Club for lunch, accompanied by the captain, tactician, and managing director of the Italian racing team. When they arrived, Tatyana, in her role as the restaurant hostess, was there to greet them.

"Mr. Bartolini, welcome!" she said in a friendly but respectful manner. "We are honored to have you here."

Bartolini was impressed that even the restaurant hostess would recognize him. In Italy everybody knew him, but this was a surprise in San Francisco. It particularly made him feel good (and important) since this was a beautiful woman.

With him, but not seated, was his bodyguard, Massimo, who stood sentry a distance away, trying not to be noticed. Massimo was the picture of an Italian bodyguard; he was a big muscular guy with shiny black hair combed straight back. He wore a purple suit and a mint green silk shirt. With his dark sunglasses, he looked like a Mafia character straight out of the movies.

When Bartolini finished lunch and was departing, Tatyana called after him, "Good luck in the Cup competition, Mr. Bartolini!"

Seeking to impress her, he turned and pointed out the big windows of the club to his yacht and said, "Can you see the name on the stern of my yacht?"

"Yes—it is *Invictus*."

"Do you know what *Invictus* means?"

"It's from the Latin, an Italian foundation language, and means *unconquerable!*"

Bartoloni was suitably impressed. Who was this fascinating woman? He wanted to continue, but had to leave for a scheduled meeting with the entire Italian America's Cup crew. As he left, he turned to her and said, "I would like to see more of you. We are having a party aboard my yacht this evening. Would you like to join us?"

"That would be delightful!"

"*Buonissimo!* Massimo will provide you the details."

That afternoon, when Nadia returned to her apartment, she reviewed the dossier on Bartolini prepared by Olga's operations staff. Roberto's family was quite prominent in Italy, and the media empire that his grandfather had founded had grown and spread across Europe. The Bartolini family estate was just outside Milan where the company headquarters were located. His mother continued to live in the house, but in an entirely separate wing, so he was afforded privacy and the ability to live his separate life.

Roberto was an only son and had lived a life of luxury from childhood. However, his father was very strict and insisted on his son getting a good education. He always expected that one day Roberto would run the company. Consequently, Roberto had attended boarding schools in Switzerland and college in the United States. Now, with his father's passing, he had inherited the company and became its CEO.

The family had holiday homes in Portofino on the Italian Riviera and on the island of Ischia off the southern coast of Italy. Roberto had been active in sailing when he was younger and continued to have an interest in sailboat racing. That had prompted him to become the sponsor of the Italian team competing for the America's Cup. Personally, he had moved up to large motor yachts.

Roberto, now forty-two years old, was still single. His father and grandfather before him had a long history of liaisons with mistresses and illicit affairs. This had led to the early demise of his father. For Roberto, an intelligent, handsome, physically fit, affluent young man, there was an abundant supply of young attractive women pursuing him constantly. Unsurprisingly this contributed to his arrogant, self-assured manner. He did enjoy women, however, and was constantly on the hunt for his next conquest. He had become somewhat bored with the "easy" ones. As with yacht racing, his race cars, and other sporting activities, the thrill of competition was a source of excitement in his life. The pursuit of conquests of interesting women had become a "sport" for him.

Nadia carefully studied everything about Bartolini: his yachting history, his escapades with women, and, in particular, the structure of his company and the various subsidiary operations that it had spread throughout the Eurozone markets. Olga's staff had thoroughly researched these matters and prepared extensive briefing materials for her. This would be helpful to her later.

That evening, as Tatyana, she arrived at the dock of the St. Francis Yacht Club where she waited with other guests for the tender for the *Invictus* to pick them up. The tender was a classic vintage Italian Riva wooden motorboat. The Riva left the dock and motored out to Bartolini's big yacht. There was a little dampness in the air that night,

*Classic Riva speed boat*

and the waves on the bay splashed against the sides of the tender as it made its passage to the big mother yacht. Tatyana took a deep breath and inhaled the smell of the fresh salt air off the bay.

The *Invictus* was a beautiful yacht. Tatyana had never seen anything like it. As she boarded the yacht on the swim step (a flat extension of a yacht near the water line on its stern to/from which people access/egress from the yacht), a steward stood waiting to greet guests. He was dressed very properly in yachting attire: navy blue pants and a white nautical jacket. He offered Tatyana and the others leaving the tender a glass of champagne.

"Welcome aboard!" the steward greeted them. "Please watch your step on the stairs leading up to the aft deck."

Tatyana walked up the stairway to the huge deck and main salon area of the yacht where the party was in full swing.

She was wearing the same black silk dress that had captivated Bernard many months before. There were two small additions: a diamond tennis bracelet and a necklace consisting of a simple white gold chain with a small diamond heart pendant. These were small indulgences that she granted herself for the big "score" on the Haussmann mission. The pendant fell strategically into the valley of her cleavage, so as to call attention to it. She had acquired a little tan during her days off, and with her new blonde hair, she looked more stunning than ever.

There were people all over the yacht, some dressed casually and some very smartly attired. She moved into the crowd, champagne in hand, but not knowing anyone. Roberto spotted her, seemingly lost in the crowd, and called her over to meet some of his friends.

Roberto kissed her on both cheeks and said, "Tatyana, I would like you to meet my friends Marco and Donatella Conti from Milano. They own a big fashion house in Milano and have a summer home on Lake Como."

Tatyana was fascinated by them and was happy to have someone interesting to talk to.

Roberto was approached by gorgeous young redhead who seemed a little miffed at the attention that he was giving to this new woman. She took him by the hand and led him away.

As the evening wore on, Tatyana met many interesting people that were there for the America's Cup series. Bartolini was nowhere to be seen and, as it grew late, she left.

The next day she received a call from Massimo.

"Would you join Mr. Bartolini for dinner tonight aboard the *Invictus?*

She, of course, accepted.

That evening she was again picked up by the yacht's tender and escorted to the *Invictus*. Sensing that this evening was an opportunity to get close to Bartolini, she entered her seductress mode. In her guise as Tatyana, she dressed fairly simply for her private dinner aboard the yacht, wearing a short black skirt and a dark red satin blouse that buttoned down the front so as to display her little diamond heart necklace. She did not wear hose since the skin on her legs displayed their beauty without embellishment. Also, as was her way, she found it unnecessary to wear a bra. Knowing that she would be boarding the *Invictus*, she wore only simple flat black shoes.

She was ready for him.

On that evening only a few crewmembers were visible. Roberto greeted her as she climbed the stairs from the swim step where the tender had dropped her off. She knew the protocol and removed her shoes, placing them in a basket on the aft deck of the yacht.

An elegant dinner was set up for them on the bridge deck (an upper deck on which the yacht is piloted). The dinner was just for the two of them. Bartolini was curious about, and aroused by, this mysterious lady. He had designs on a "special evening" with her. He was sure that she would "stay the night," as his other lady friend guests would always do.

Music from the Italian opera *Turandot* was playing on the yacht's sound system.

*How appropriate!* she thought, knowing that, in the opera, the prince wins the hand of the cold princess by solving three riddles. She speculated that her prince, Roberto, would not be that lucky this evening.

Roberto had thought most of the day about how he would seduce Tatyana … how he would set his trap. It was a very familiar scheme. It would be a lovely dinner, in a setting young women simply dream about: dining aboard an impressive private yacht with a young, rich, handsome man. An expensive wine that cost as much as a month of her income would accompany their dinner. There would be a plentiful amount of it for her to drink in order to loosen up any of her inhibitions, if she had any. Romantic music was programmed on the yacht's sound system.

He had done this many times before and it *always worked*. For this evening he had a new target in Tatyana and had high expectations for an enjoyable evening. Of course he could easily have any of his usual beauties, but this new girl intrigued him. She seemed very different. From her accent, he believed that she might be Eastern European or, more likely, Russian. Apparently she was smart and knew a lot about him and the Cup competition. It could not have been easy for her to get the job as hostess at the St. Francis Yacht Club. He had become somewhat bored with the other women, and this promised to be a more interesting conquest.

*Ah, it's going to be an unfair contest,* he mused. *She is a simple young woman of modest means who surely aspires to win my affections. If things go well she probably thinks she can marry into wealth. Hah! This fragile female will be easy prey for me.*

Roberto greeted her as she walked up the stairs from the swim step to the main deck on the stern of the yacht. He offered her a glass of champagne. "I believe you will enjoy this."

Roberto was the image of what most women would die for. He was incredibly handsome, almost too perfect. Most Latinos tan easily, and he was no exception. He had dark eyes and long wavy black hair that was meticulously groomed. He was wearing a navy blue blazer with a light blue pocket square. With a crisp white shirt and gray slacks, he looked like a model straight out of *GQ Magazine*. He was dressed to kill. To Tatyana this all seemed too obvious… too contrived.

"Would you like a tour of the boat before dinner?"

"Of course! I would love to get a full tour of your *toy* boat, Mr. Bartolini," she said.

The *Invictus* was an impressive boat, unlike anything she had ever dreamed existed. She had seen only a small part of it during Roberto's party and was anxious to enjoy the rest.

"Let's start at the areas near the stern of the yacht on the lower deck and work our way forward," he said.

Roberto guided her down the stairs to the swim step and entered what Roberto called the garage. The transom of the yacht had huge doors that opened up into an area where the tender was stowed when the yacht was under way. It also contained the yacht's "water toys" such as wave runners, water skis, scuba gear, and other items that Tatyana did not recognize. There was also a gym that opened into the garage when the tender was deployed. Off to one side was a cabin that Roberto explained was the living quarters for the yacht's chief engineer.

From the garage there was a door leading into the engine room. He showed her in.

"I'm sure it's not interesting to a lady, but let me show you the engine room anyway."

It was not what Tatyana expected. It was mostly painted white and was as pristine as a pharmaceutical manufacturing plant. Roberto pointed to the two large 2,500 HP Caterpillar engines that powered the yacht. The room also contained all the mechanical equipment to operate the boat—generators, fresh water makers, and other items necessary for it to be self-sufficient on a trans-oceanic voyage.

"Let's go back up to the main deck," he suggested. "You saw most of this at the party on Saturday: the large aft deck, the main salon, and dining room. But let me show you the galley and the master stateroom."

As they moved back up to the main deck, Roberto described the *Invictus* as a Feadship built in 2007.

"She is 245 feet long overall and maintains a full complement of twenty-two crewmembers when cruising with guests. There are six guest staterooms all set up for adults. The yacht's cruising speed is 14 knots and she has a trans-oceanic range."

Passing through the main salon, Tatyana could not help notice the extraordinary cabinetwork that seemed pervasive throughout the yacht. It integrated into the structures what appeared to be mahogany, teak, and other exotic woods that she had only read about but never seen.

They arrived at the galley. There was a middle-aged man at the cooktop and a young woman chopping away at vegetables, both obviously at work preparing their dinner.

"Let me introduce you to the master chef of the *Invictus*. Giovanni! This is Tatyana, our guest for this evening."

Giovanni was obviously Italian. He was slender, for a man of his profession, had a dark, well-trimmed beard, and was wearing an apron and a small chef's hat.

"Mr. Bartolini. She is a pretty one!" he said in Italian, looking her up and down, not thinking that Tatyana understood the language.

She just smiled, pretending not to understand his comment.

"Giovanni will prepare a superb dinner for us this evening," Roberto said. "He makes the best pasta in Italy, but tonight we will have something more elegant." Roberto continued, "He has a staff of six and a purser that supports him when we are cruising with guests aboard. The chef is perhaps the most important crewmember, other than the captain. When we are cruising with a full complement of crew and guests, his task is challenging. We might have twelve guests and twenty-two crewmembers. That's thirty-four people who need to be fed three meals each day. He has to plan that out and procure all the supplies in advance of what is often a two-week cruise itinerary. Even with a sizable galley crew to help him, it is a daunting task, and I am amazed that nothing ever seems to go wrong. Now let me show you my quarters," he said, walking toward the bow of the yacht.

The master stateroom was large, spanning the complete width of the beam of the yacht. It included an office, walk-in closet, and a large bathroom area complete with his and hers dressing areas. It was beautifully appointed in marble.

"Where are the guest quarters?" Tatyana asked.

"The guest staterooms and crew quarters are on the lower deck. The crew quarters are forward in the bow area on that deck."

"Let's go top-side."

There was an elevator mid-ship, but they instead took the stairs to the bridge deck. Tatyana went first, with Roberto following. He gazed at her shapely legs as she moved up the stairs ahead of him. He marveled at her provocative svelte body and felt a surge of uncontrollable lust. There was a certain natural beauty to her skin that was not compromised by one who might have worn hose. He thought, *What a sexy lady!*

On the bridge deck there was a good-sized lounge and bar area, with a game table and a wonderful outside dining area toward the stern. Toward the bow of the yacht was the bridge, from which the Invictus was piloted. Tatyana marveled at all the navigation and instrumentation equipment. It was very high-tech, like what she imagined a control room to be for a large ship or the cockpit of an airliner. Just aft of the bridge was a stateroom and office for the captain.

"There is one more level," said Roberto as they climbed to the sky deck. The views from the sky deck were grand. There was a bar, several lounge chairs, and a Jacuzzi.

"I am impressed!" Tatyana exclaimed.

Hoping to keep things moving along, Roberto wanted to get on with the evening and his agenda. "I'm famished. Giovanni is probably ready for us. Dinner is being served on the bridge deck."

As they returned to the outside area just off the bridge deck lounge, Tatyana was stunned by the setting. There, an elegant private table was set up for the two of them. It was covered with a simple white tablecloth, but the dishes, silverware, and wine glasses were fabulous. It was topped off with fresh flowers and candlelight.

It was a beautiful summer night looking across the water at the lights of the city. One could not want for a more romantic setting.

A moment later a stewardess appeared with the drinks. "Mr. Bartolini, I believe this is what you requested," she remarked respectfully.

"I think this is the perfect aperitif to get our evening started," he responded.

As they were seated, the stewardess served them each a small glass of a premier vodka. It was ice cold, and there was a coat of frost on the glasses.

"Perhaps you are Russian and might enjoy this as a starter," Roberto said, introducing it.

Tatyana nodded knowingly and lifted her glass in a toasting gesture.

She could not help note an air of extreme self-confidence about Roberto. He knew that he would have his way with her that evening. His eyes moved capriciously across Tatyana's body... like a tiger checking out its prey before devouring it. Even without him touching her, she felt violated by his visual inspection of her anatomy. Would she survive this evening... his potent advances? It remained to be seen.

*Who is seducing who tonight?* she wondered.

At dinner, he questioned her about her background and heritage. He wanted to know more about her, but she was the most aggressive interrogator. She asked about his many business operations in a flattering way, and he was only too accommodating to answer in order to impress her further. Of course, Tatyana already knew all about him and did not need to learn more through this line of inquiry. It was simply staged to allow him to impress her... to bring his guard down.

As they finished the dinner, a stewardess appeared with an after-dinner drink. "Mr. Bartolini, I believe you requested a port to follow your food service."

So there they were in that romantic setting, sipping a glass of fine Port wine, gazing at the lights of San Francisco reflecting across the water.

As Tatyana leaned over to touch her glass to his in a toast, she thanked him for a lovely evening. Her blouse opened a little and the diamond heart on her necklace moved gently across the valley of her tanned bosom.

As his ardor surged, he thought, *I have to have her tonight!*

Then came Roberto's proposition. "You are a very beautiful woman. I would like you to spend the night."

Nadia was not surprised. She had expected it to come to this.

"You are an attractive man, but I have only known you for one day. So I must respectfully decline."

He was stunned! No woman ever turned him down.

"What can I do to get you to stay? I can make this a very pleasant experience for you."

"Roberto, let me be clear. I am not staying the night on the *Invictus*!" she strongly asserted.

Undeterred, he tried a different angle.

"You seem like an adventurous type. Poker is a popular game these days. What say we play a high-stakes game? Each of us will get $10,000 in chips and play until one of us wins or loses all of their chips. If you win, you keep the winnings, $20,000. If I win, you stay the night."

"I must warn you," Tatyana said confidently. "I am rather good at games and have played poker enough to develop a respectable skill at it. Are you sure that you want to lose all that money?"

Roberto was delighted to hear her cocky response. He was certain that she was over-confident and that he could easily beat her. *Poker is a man's game*, he thought.

"You are on! I hope that you like sleeping on a yacht."

They moved inside to the yacht's sky lounge where there was a game table. A steward, who seemed British from his accent, brought them another drink. It was another ice-cold vodka, like the one served at the beginning of the evening.

"Are you trying to take advantage of me?" Nadia asked in a subdued, demure voice. "This is the second high potency vodka that you have served. I am Russian and can handle it, but you may lose your edge in the poker match."

"We will see. Let's get into the game," he said.

Turning to the steward, Roberto asked, "Rogers, would you mind serving as the dealer for our card game?"

"It would be my pleasure," he responded. "Sir, what game will you be playing?"

"We will play Texas Hold-em, if that's okay with the lady."

"I've never been to Texas, but I know the game, and that will be fine," she responded.

In the early hands of the poker match, the level of bets was low. Roberto was "a player" and was drawing her into his trap. The size of the bets started to move up. There was a fairly good size pot when Roberto pressed her with an increased bet that would have taken most of her chips. She looked down at her hole cards—the face-down cards that the holder isn't obliged to reveal until the showdown—at what was certain to be a winning hand. It was too early for her to win, and she wanted to egg him on. So, she folded. Roberto revealed his hand. He had been bluffing!

"You fooled me!" she exclaimed. "You had me completely convinced that you had the winning hand."

In the next hand Tatyana had poor cards. She decided to bluff him and lose … so she could portray herself as a novice. It worked, and Roberto collected a moderate size pot. He thought to himself, *I am going to have a good time tonight.*

After a few unexciting hands, the winnings went back and forth. The match stood about even. Then Roberto drew a very good hand. As play progressed, the bets grew larger. Roberto was convinced that Tatyana was bluffing again. She seemed a little tentative in her bets at first, as if unsure of herself. He was reading her body language to gauge the strength of her position. A novice, he knew, would not know to avoid telegraphing the strength or weakness of their hand.

Roberto noticed Nadia playing with her little garnet ring. She twisted it and tapped it nervously.

"What's with the ring?" he asked.

"Oh, nothing!" she murmured.

"It doesn't go with your diamond pendant and bracelet," he said in a critical tone. "It looks very inexpensive. Why do you wear it? If you stay the night, I will buy you a much nicer one."

"I don't *want* a nicer one," she said shortly. "This was my first piece of jewelry, and it has a special meaning."

Roberto responded contemptuously. "I think that a classy woman like you should not be wearing such a cheap ring."

"It brings me good luck," she professed.

Roberto cocked his eyebrows skeptically. "Surely you do not believe that. You will need a lot of luck to beat me in this game."

Tatyana became aware that the opera music from *Turandot* in the background was commencing the famous final act aria, "Nessun Dorma," at just this auspicious moment. In the opera an unknown prince must solve three riddles to win Princess Turandot's hand in marriage. If he fails he will lose his head. Of course he solves the riddles; then, because she still resists, he challenges the princess to discover his name by morning or she must relent. As she cannot discover his name, he exclaims, "*Vincerò!*" meaning, "I will win!"

Tatyana thought, *This prince is going to be very disappointed tonight!*

As more cards were drawn, Tatyana began to bet more aggressively, making him wonder, *Perhaps she has a hand that she thinks might win!* When the river card—the last card to be drawn at the end of a hand—came up, he was now certain that he had the winning hand. Roberto had two aces as his hole cards. There was one ace, two deuces, a seven, and a ten on the "community" board. His aces-over-deuces full house was a certain winner.

This was an ideal situation for him. By her betting pattern, he was sure that she had a good hand and was confident that she could win. She was tentative at first, but had increased her bets when the seven and ten had come out for the community cards. He reasoned that she probably had two sevens or two tens as hole cards and thought her full house would win. Also there were three spades on the community board. Perhaps she had a flush, thinking it to be a winner. She certainly did not suspect that he was holding two aces. His skill as an experienced player had allowed him to read her body language and betting pattern.

He thought, *Now is the time to move in for the kill ... and get on to the bedroom.* So he pushed all of his chips into the pot.

"All in!" he exclaimed ... in a move to end and win the game. A cocksure grin spread across his face.

She leaned across the table, again tantalizing him with her cleavage.

"I call!" she said with a certain sly conviction.

*I have her!* he thought, and with a confident gesture of showmanship, he turned over his cards showing the two aces.

"*Vincerò! Vincerò!* I win!" proclaimed Roberto, the unconquerable master of the *Invicus.*

Tatyana looked at him across the table with those deep blue, probing eyes. Roberto felt her looking directly into his eyes. It was unnerving, as if her vision was penetrating deep inside his soul. She turned over her hole cards.

"I have two pair ... *of deuces!*"

With the two on the community board, she had *quad* deuces!

Her words, spoken in perfect Italian, came like a dagger. "*Non penso così. Mi dovete venti mila dollari!*" ("I don't think so! You owe me twenty grand!")

Roberto was devastated. Had she been clever enough to send him false body language ... to act unsure of her bets? At the time of the "flop" when the first three cards were turned over on the board, she had to know that she had an unbeatable hand. Yet she had acted tentatively, as if she was unsure of herself. It seemed unbelievable that she had so cleverly duped him; that she had enticed him into her trap with no sign that she might have him beat.

Even after this humiliation, he did not want her to leave. Now he *really* wanted her badly. As Rogers picked up the cards and was leaving, Roberto leaned over and whispered to her, "Okay, you won the poker match. But I will pay you another fifty grand to stay the night."

She looked at him intently. He felt her dark blue eyes penetrating him once again, as if playing with him. It was uncanny, as if those piercing eyes were probing deep inside him, looking for something ... seeing everything.

"Absolutely no! You cannot *buy* me... but perhaps you can *earn* me."

*What did she mean "earn me?"* he pondered.

Tatyana knew that it would turn into a one-night stand, and he would be done with her. She had bigger designs on him. Roberto now felt a knot in his stomach as he realized that he was going to go "unfulfilled" that night.

"I want a rematch!" he demanded, pounding the gaming table with his fist.

He was searching for any angle to get to her. He could not let this one get away.

This was what Nadia wanted—an opportunity to get him deeper into her clutches.

"Tomorrow!" he proposed.

"I'm sorry," she replied. "There is a dinner event at the Club tomorrow, and I have to work late. How about Thursday?"

"Yes, let's do it!" he exclaimed.

So the rematch was set.

That Thursday evening, Roberto again arranged a romantic dinner before they would play again. He was an outstanding poker player and certain that she had just got lucky. Roberto was a reasonably intelligent man, but he had *no idea* what he was up against. With her soft, quiet manner, she would not raise any suspicion. But underneath it all was a woman that was vastly superior to him mentally. During dinner, conversation again turned to his company and the broad range of media businesses in his empire.

She asked if he had any business units in the rapidly growing arena of online social media. He said that he did not, but was watching it. Tatyana reminded him that San Francisco was very near Silicon Valley where much of the social media phenomenon was taking off.

"It would be interesting to meet some of the entrepreneurs in this emerging industry, but I have no contacts in the area," Bartolini said.

"Perhaps I can help. Through the Club, I have met a few of the key people from down in the Valley, where they are involved in the tech industry. With your extensive businesses, especially in Europe, perhaps they might see the potential for a strategic relationship."

To Roberto this sounded intriguing ... but he was on a mission to seduce this woman. The Internet social media idea offered an opportunity to continue the quest.

They played the poker rematch later that evening, and, again, he lost. Not only did he lose, she had completely outsmarted him in the game.

Bartolini was becoming totally obsessed with "conquering" this lady, but was not having much luck with the poker deal. It had begun to dawn on him that Tatyana was no ordinary woman ... it was beginning to dawn on him that he might have underestimated her. In a strange way, her high intelligence added to his sexual desire for her. It made her a more interesting and intriguing target for his advances.

But he knew very little about this mysterious female. *Who is she?* he wondered. When he had asked Tatyana about her background, she had been evasive and turned the conversation back to him.

He was busy with America's Cup preparations in the days that followed, but Tatyana had not tried to reach him. He was used to women pursuing him. She wasn't. Maybe she was not a "gold digger" like the rest.

He decided to take the next step, so he initiated a call to her. He expressed an interest in the Silicon Valley social media idea and told her that he would like to meet some of the people, if she could arrange it.

"Let me work on it, and I'll get back to you," Tatyana responded.

The "sting" was beginning to develop. Tatyana needed to strategize with Olga.

Olga flew up to San Francisco to meet with Tatyana and plan their next move. Tatyana had met some of the leaders in some rapidly growing Internet companies and had learned of one that was media oriented. That company, Xanda Media, Inc., needed to raise money to finance their growth. She thought about the huge amount of money flowing into these start-up private companies and thought that there was a way for her and Olga to get their hands on some of that money. But she needed some legal help.

Olga told Tatyana that she had an attorney that worked for her; that he knew how to work around the formalities and get things done. He was a little shady, but had worked for her for a long time and was very skillful in helping her *agents* "close deals." Tatyana just needed to convince Roberto to invest in the Internet media company.

Tatyana called the CEO of Xanda Media, a nerdy young man, all of twenty-six years old. His father was a member of the St. Francis Yacht Club and, together with a few others, had put up all the money to get the company going. It was at the yacht club that she had met them. Now the company had about twenty-five young software engineers working day and night at the company, many of them unpaid. The young CEO, Cyrus Moore, had no business experience but was on to a big idea that promised to revolutionize the big parts of the media industry.

Tatyana was able to arrange a number of company visits for Roberto with Internet companies that were further along in their progress. When the subject of investment and valuation came up, the numbers were so high that Roberto thought them to be outrageous. Also, none of these had any significant synergy with his enterprise.

Tatyana called Roberto and suggested that they visit Xanda Media.

"Roberto, I think there is a younger company that would be a good fit for you. They are doing some very innovative work in the media space. Perhaps, even, there is a fit with your own business."

"When can we go see them?"

"They are desperate for money, so I believe I can set it up as early as tomorrow."

"Set it up for two pm tomorrow, if you can, and I will have my driver pick us up just after one o'clock."

Tatyana was able to set up the meeting. The next day Tatyana met

Roberto at the yacht club, and his driver, Hans, arrived to take them down the peninsula to the Silicon Valley location of Xanda Media. Hans was a very sophisticated man of German heritage. He had graying hair and was dressed in a black suit, white shirt, and tie. He greeted her politely and opened the door for her to enter the black town car that Roberto had under contract during his stay in the Bay Area.

As they drove out of the city and down Highway 101, Tatyana briefed Roberto on the company.

"Xanda Media is about two years old, but has been pioneering some amazing developments in the media industry. I think you will find them interesting. This will be a different kind of company environment than you have ever experienced. Do not let the apparent disorganization and youth of the team mislead you. This company is 'hot.' Many investors want a piece of their action."

They arrived at the company's facility in Redwood City and were greeted by the company's young CEO. Tatyana introduced them.

"Mr. Bartolini, I would like you to meet Cyrus Moore."

"Welcome Mr. Bartolini, " he said. "Tatyana has told me a lot about your company. It seems that we have a common interest. Let me show you what we are doing."

In the lobby, the receptionist asked, "Please sign the visitor register, if you please."

Roberto was very impressed with what he saw in Xanda's operations. In this small office facility, there were computers everywhere and young software engineers working around the clock. Many slept and ate there for days on end. In his discussions with Cyrus he could see the potential of the business. Importantly, there was a big synergy with his media empire.

Xanda Media needed financing to take their company to the next level, and they were running out of money. So there was an urgency for them to raise capital. When Cyrus and Roberto talked about what their two businesses might do together, ideas flowed with enthusiasm. Cyrus could see that with financing and with a deal with this big European media company, Xanda might be able to go public next year. They might be able to get a valuation of a billion dollars, or more, based on the valuations of other Internet companies in their space.

However, they needed money and needed it fast before the whole thing blew up. When Roberto had signed into their guest log on his arrival, he noticed above his signature on the visitor log the name of a Google executive, and above it the name of a partner of a big venture capital firm. He could not have known that Tatyana had written those names on the roster earlier that day. He feared that they could get the deal before him.

They talked at length about the company on their drive back up to the city.

"Do you know what they need and what part of the company I would be able to get for the investment?" Roberto asked.

Tatyana then outlined the basics of what she had been told. "They need $30 million to finance their growth through the next two years. Because they are about to run out of money, if you are prepared to act quickly, I am told that you could buy half of the company for that amount. But there are other interested parties pursuing this deal."

With a little quick math, he saw the possibility of making perhaps a half billion dollars within two years. Still, he was uncomfortable. He had just met the company and had not had his staff do any due diligence on the business. The next morning he conducted a conference call with his CFO and strategic planning staff. They charged into an expedited due diligence review. Xanda's business plan and financial statements were transmitted back to his headquarters in Milan. Roberto's planning staff immediately saw the potential of a joint venture with this young start-up technology company. The business plan showed how it could grow rapidly, especially with what the two companies could do together.

Roberto's CFO reviewed Xanda's financial statements and found nothing alarming. As might be expected, it was simply a young, high growth company losing a lot of money at this early stage of its development. As a precaution he called the company's account-ing, tax, and audit firm. Nothing they said led him to question their legitimacy. His legal staff checked the California records and confirmed the existence of Xanda Media, Inc. It was a legitimately formed corporation. Everything seemed in order.

With this report in hand, Roberto called Tatyana and said that he would like to proceed with the investment.

"Can we get in this deal before Google or the venture capitalists?"

"I believe they would prefer to do the deal with you because of the strategic potential of a relationship with your company," Tatyana explained.

She said that she would talk to Cyrus and attempt to get expedited financing documents prepared.

Xanda Media really did not have any good legal counsel. Everything to date had been done by a family attorney. She told Roberto that she wanted to make sure that everything would be properly done.

"Through my contacts I know of a top corporate attorney in Los Angeles that can turn around the documents fast and make certain that everything is in order according to US corporate law," Tatyana told Roberto, knowing he was preoccupied with prepara-tions for the initial America's Cup trials and hoped he wouldn't question her. "If you wish, I will coordinate with Cyrus and the LA law firm and get back to you as soon as possible."

"I would be grateful if you could facilitate that process," he said, but in the back of his mind he thought, *What in hell is a yacht club hostess doing in the middle of a corporate finance deal?*

There was another deal point that he wanted to discuss with her.

"Tatyana, I am very grateful for what you are doing for me. If this deal closes, I intend to pay you a fee of $250,000 for finding it and for your assistance in getting the deal done."

"That's a lot of money to me. It's completely unexpected. Thank you!" she responded appreciatively.

He was not finished. "There is one other thing. When the deal closes, I would like to have a private celebration with you. I want you to stay overnight with me on the *Invictus*."

"I guess it's about time for us. You have a deal!" she relented.

The financing documents arrived in two days and everything was in order. Tatyana had run them down to the San Mateo office of Xanda Media and obtained the enthusiastic signature of Cyrus and others. Roberto was going over the final docs and noticed one small abnormality. The company name on the financing agreements was Xanda Media, *Ltd.*, not *Inc.* He called the attorney at the LA law firm of Milcass & McNab that had prepared the documents and asked about that detail. The attorney, James Bishop, had given Roberto his private number so he could call him directly and reach him whenever he wished.

"Counselor Bishop, there appears to be a mistake in the financing documents," Roberto said. "The company is Xanda Media, *incorporated*, not *limited*."

Bishop responded, advising him, "Mr. Bartolini, The *limited* entity is a holding company for Xanda Media, Inc., which is a 100 percent-owned subsidiary."

He referred Roberto to the Reps and Warrantees section of the financing agreement where it was so stated. Roberto was satisfied and signed the documents.

He called his Milan office and faxed a copy of the closing docs with instructions to wire transfer the funds into the account, for which instructions had been provided. He received confirmation the next day that the transaction had closed, and that the funds were transferred according to the directions.

He called Tatyana to congratulate her and set up their celebration dinner and night together. She was overjoyed and said that he could look forward to *a night that he would never forget*.

It was another warm beautiful night on San Francisco Bay. The *Invictus* was all lit up and prepared for Tatyana's arrival. Roberto had placed a check for $250,000 on the bed where he would, at last, consummate this deal. His shore boat waited patiently at the dock. On this night there were no other guests.

The time for her arrival came and went. It was not like her to be late. He wondered if she had a problem. He called her apartment, but no one answered. He called the St. Francis Yacht Club and was told she had resigned earlier that day. With the prospect of picking up a $250,000 check that evening, perhaps he could understand. Still, he began to be concerned. Something was not quite right.

He decided to call Cyrus. Perhaps she had gone down to celebrate with the young entrepreneurs before coming to the yacht. Cyrus told him that she was not there and asked when the money might hit their bank account. Roberto said that it had been transferred the day before and should be there. He would check with his bank ASAP.

It was now 5:00 am in Milan, but he had a night number for a bank officer because of the size of dealings that his company had with it. The bank confirmed that the funds had been sent. He was perplexed and called Cyrus back, assuring him that the funds had been transferred to the account of Xanda's holding company in Bermuda. For a moment there was silence on the other end.

"Xanda does not have a holding company; we are a simple C Corporation," Cyrus replied.

There was a long pause on the other end on the line, as Roberto began to suspect that something had gone wrong, very wrong.

"I will get back to you."

This was becoming very worrisome. He called his corporate counsel in Milan and asked him to check on a Bermuda-based firm by the name of Xanda Media, Ltd., as soon as possible in the morning. The next day his corporate counsel would report back that the company had existed, but had been disbanded and its bank accounts closed. He also decided to call the attorney, James Bishop, on his private line to ask about it. When he called there was a message: "This number has been disconnected and there is no new number."

He called directory assistance in LA and asked for the main number for the Milcass & McNab law firm, and then called it. He reached one of the attorneys working late and asked for the new number for James Bishop, the attorney that had been helping him. On the other end of the line there was a pause; then came the answer, "We do not have any lawyer working here by that name."

Now he knew for sure that Tatyana was not coming. It occurred to him that the St. Francis Yacht Club had her employment information, including her Social Security and driver's license numbers. From there he could track her down. He was eventually to learn later that those numbers belonged to a woman that had left the country over a year earlier.

Roberto thought back to the first time that he met Tatyana and how she had commented on the name of his yacht: *Invictus*.

Somehow its meaning, "*unconquerable*," had lost some of its virtue.

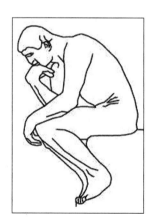

# CHAPTER 8

# INTERMEZZO

NADIA WAS BACK AT THE SAN Ysidro Ranch. She loved the place, and it was a good environment for her to relax and read after a big assignment. She walked down the hill to the cottage where guests check in. She remembered that they had a library there for those guests looking for something interesting to read. As she examined the books there, she came across a first edition of *Doctor Zhivago*. *What a treasure!* she thought. This first edition was published in Russian. Only a few copies existed, and it was miraculous that the San Ysidro Ranch had one and that she was holding it.

*First edition printed in Russian*

Nadia remembered the story of its origins. The author, Boris Pastermak, had been awarded the Nobel Prize in literature, but came under extreme pressure in communist Russia and never collected the prize money. He had been persecuted severely by the KGB and threatened that his mistress would be sent to the Gulag prison if he traveled to Stockholm.

Tucking the book safely under her arm, she returned to her cottage. A handyman had made a fire in her fireplace and she settled into a comfortable chair to read. She was intrigued with the story of a man torn between his love for two different women—his wife and his mistress—at a troubled time in communist Russian history. Although she had never known love herself, she enjoyed reading romance novels.

The next morning, her phone rang. It was Olga.

"Nadia, I am working on the beginnings of a major project. It will take months of training and preparation. I want you to come back to the Malibu house and work in the events company for a while during your preparation for the assignment.

"Also, this can be a time for you to learn more about men. You need to understand them at a deeper level; to be able to get inside their psyche; to understand their emotions, their drives, and their complete behavioral makeup. In short, you must know everything that makes them tick: what they care about and how they make decisions.

"Up to now you have only known a few men well: your two former husbands. They are not representative of the circles that you will be traveling in for the rest of your career and life. Bernard Haussmann and Roberto Bartolini are more like the men you will encounter— more complex, well-educated, and well-traveled; more sophisticated and perhaps somewhat chauvinistic. However, your experiences with them were only brief interludes.

"It is essential as you take on assignments at a higher level that you understand intimately the many complex layers of the targets that we pursue. Alexandra has taught you many of the technical skills about how to give men pleasure of a physical kind. She is a master at it, so I am confident that you have learned her methods well. You know how to tease the male species and entice them into your trap.

"But, if we are to remake you into a lethal weapon in the arena of big game hunting, you must elevate the full dimension of your skills and expertise to be effective with the world's wealthiest and most powerful men."

"I am more than equal to the challenge," said Nadia confidently.

"Of that I am certain," Olga replied. "You will come back to the Malibu house, then partner up with Alexandra for a while. Meet the other agents there and learn what you can from them. Also, take a bigger role in the events management company. It will provide you exposure to our major clients and to a range of accomplished men.

"In a couple of weeks' time there will be an important political fundraiser for Senator Barry Wheeler. All the power players in LA will be there. I can arrange for you to attend as a guest. We will provide you with a new identity so you can mix with that crowd.

"While none of these attendees will have met you before, you may have to deal with them in the future, so I want you to stay with your blonde look for a while."

"Is there any chance that Bernard Haussmann will be there?" Nadia asked in a concerned voice.

"No, I have checked the guest list and his office. He is traveling in Europe on an extended trip," Olga assured her.

*That's a relief,* Nadia thought. "What is it you want me to accomplish?"

"For this event there is no defined mission," Olga said. "I just want you to mix socially with people at this level and get comfortable with it."

Olga also told Nadia that she had laid out a reading program for her to familiarize her with the public policy issues that were likely to be discussed at the event. Nadia was a voracious reader and looked forward to this aspect of her preparation.

Olga described Nadia's new identity. "You will assume the persona of Elena Sinclair. You will be the widow of a young Internet billionaire who died in a fatal crash when he lost control of his Lamborghini, colliding with a concrete abutment on the freeway.

"Since your husband had been reclusive and maintained a low profile in the tech industry, no one would have known him or his company. You were a software engineer in his company and had met him through your employment. A romance followed, and you had become married. The company had been engaged in advanced technology work on cyber security. A year before the accident he had sold the company to Science Applications International Corporation, commonly referred to as SAIC, a large, secretive contract research firm. SAIC conducts many projects for DARPA, the Defense Advanced Research Projects Agency; NSA, The National Security Agency; and the CIA.

"Owing to your fictitious husband's business, you will profess to have a keen interest in Internet security and the growing threat of cyber warfare. What you learn about Internet security may be helpful in your next real mission. The necessary materials will be provided to you. That is all."

The line went dead.

Nadia returned to Olga's Malibu estate and immersed herself in the material. Because Nadia loved to read, she spent all of her available hours learning about the current public policy issues ... and importantly about the nefarious hacker attacks on the US financial system and the national security risk that they posed.

She also worked on the events management projects and had social time to share with Alexandra and some of the other women-agents at the Malibu house. It was a pretty easygoing time in her life, a nice break from the intense mission-focused assignments that she had run. While she enjoyed this period, she was anxious to get back into the intriguing agenda that Olga was planning for her.

The time for the political fundraiser for Senator Wheeler was fast approaching. Nadia needed something appropriate to wear. Her silk dresses were not adequate for the role of a woman of means—they were too simple and too sexy.

She asked Alexandra, who knew her way around the shops on Rodeo Drive, to help. She said that it would be fun to do a girls' dress up day. Nadia knew nothing about fashion and was very uncomfortable spending money on such frivolous things. Her impoverished existence as a youth still gripped tightly on her attitudes.

Even in Beverly Hills, the statuesque blonde Alexandra and Nadia turned heads as they strolled down the street, window shopping and stopping in the boutiques to find something for Nadia's incarnation as Elena Sinclair. They stopped at the Il Fornaio Restaurant for lunch, sharing an order of angel hair pasta with a simple marinara sauce and a glass of Brunello di Montalcino.

During lunch their conversation inevitably turned to men.

"Nadia, have you ever been in love?" Alexandra asked.

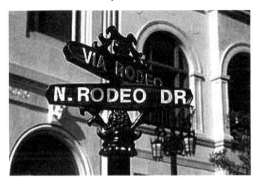

Nadia's wholesomely pretty face clouded with sadness. "No, I'm afraid that particular part of life has escaped me. All of my relationships with men have been out of necessity, not choice. I envy you, Alex, for the romance that you have in your life, but for me, every relationship that I have had with men has been an unpleasant experience. Also, I must admit that affection is difficult for me. I have read about romance in novels, but have never come close to experiencing it."

"That's too bad, Nadia; I am sorry for you. I am a hopeless romantic and can easily fall for any attractive man that I meet," Alexandra said. "I get excited and love every aspect of my experiences with men. I can't get enough of it."

"Alexandra, how do you know what true love is?" Nadia asked, almost pleadingly. "How can you distinguish between infatuation driven by passion and a genuine, strong affection that a man might have for you? Physical pleasure can come easy … but how do you know that a man is interested in you as a person? It must be difficult for an attractive young woman like you."

Alexandra furrowed her brow in thought. "It's hard to explain. If you have not experienced a really great romance, there is no way I can help you understand fully how to recognize it. It's not just about sex or companionship. Sex is about giving and getting physical pleasure with your man. It should not be confused with love.

"In many ways *a kiss* is a far more loving encounter between a man and a woman. It is an intimate expression of the ultimate affection. It is easy for me to enjoy sex with a man, whether or not I'm in love with him.

"But with a man I love, *a kiss* is the ultimate expression of my passion for him. It is a thrill to be embraced by a man who loves you … to feel the strength of his muscular body as he pulls you close to him … to feel his touch as he caresses your body with desire … and to engage him in a passionate kiss. It is a real turn-on!"

"You are very fortunate, Alexandra," Nadia sighed. "I have never been kissed by a man, other than as a prelude to sex. It is difficult for me to let go emotionally in a relationship. Men often see me as a somewhat cold woman. I wonder what it would be like for me to have a real romance."

"Your struggle with affection is understandable because of your difficult start in life," said Alex, placing a sympathetic hand on Nadia's arm. "It will come to you naturally when you meet the right man. You need to be patient and let love in when it comes to you."

She paused and asked, "Wouldn't you someday like to get married and have children?"

"That is difficult for me to even think about," Nadia said. "My own parents abandoned me at birth. I only have bad memories from my childhood. I have never known love or even affection. Because of that, I do not see myself as a mother with children. I have an exciting life now. Perhaps love and romance do not have a place in my life."

"That would be regrettable," said Alexandra affectionately. "In time, perhaps that will change. You are a beautiful lady and much lies ahead for you in life."

After lunch they continued to shop. At the Armani shop, Nadia found a dress in her favorite sapphire blue color. It was a fairly simple style in silk, like her black one, and would flatter her figure and match her eye color. Alexandra advised her against it, arguing that she needed something more appropriate for the wealthy widow role that she would be playing.

They moved further down the street to the Valentino boutique and found a dress that Alexandra loved.

"Valentino is known for their haute couture fashions in their signature color, red," Alexandra said, displaying her fashion savvy.

Nadia's taste, ran to the conservative side, but the dress that Alexandra had picked out for her was in a more flamboyant Valentino style.

"I know this style does not appeal to you, but try it on," Alexandra encouraged her.

Shrugging, Nadia did try it on and had to admit the girl that smiled back at her in the mirror looked stunning. It was a little too flamboyant for her taste but Alexandra was excited and thought it was perfect.

"Alex, I respect your expertise in such matters, so I will get this dress for the senator's fundraiser, but I also want the blue one that we saw back at Armani for a future occasion."

Excited and pleased, Alexandra jumped up and down like a schoolgirl. She ran to Nadia and spontaneously hugged her. Nadia paused for a moment, not knowing how to respond … and then slowly put her arms around Alexandra and hugged her back.

Nadia could not remember ever being hugged by another person. True, she had often been embraced by a sexually motivated male. But this was different. This hug was an affectionate expression of caring by a friend. It felt good to her, and the thought that someone could be that happy for her was a new, warming sensation—something that she had missed in her life up to this point.

With no family or person that had ever cared for her, Nadia had always lived with a shadow of loneliness over her. Sarah, back in Bryansk, had been the lone exception. With Alexandra, Olga, and *the agency*, she was at last experiencing a feeling of belonging and an emotional connection to others. She was beginning to experience some happiness.

Nadia bought both dresses.

"Now we need to get you some shoes and a handbag!" Alexandra exclaimed. She was on a mission. "Neiman Marcus is just down the street, and they have a great selection. Yesterday, I saw a pair of red, lizard-print, leather high heels by Jimmy Choo there. They would be perfect with the Valentino dress. We can probably also find you a nice matching handbag."

"Alex, you are too much!" laughed Nadia. "You really go all out, don't you? I am getting tired, but let's make that one last stop before we head home."

After the Neiman Marcus stop, Nadia was exhausted, and their shopping day came to an end. As they drove back to the Malibu house, Nadia thought deeply about the feeling of another person, Alexandra, caring sincerely for her. Small as it was, it was a wonderful feeling.

After they returned to the Malibu house, Olga went to her vault and lent Nadia a stunning diamond necklace, bracelet, and ring for the evening. The Valentino dress buttoned down the front, presenting a perfect landscape for Nadia's neckline and the contours of her breasts ... and for the beautiful necklace. With Olga's jewelry, Nadia would certainly look the part of the widow of a billionaire.

The fundraiser was a black tie affair at the venerable Beverly Hills Hotel on Sunset Boulevard. The Beverly Hills Hotel was opened in 1912 and, over the years, had become the iconic meeting place for movie industry celebrities, business leaders, and international VIPs. The event was to be held in the hotel's Crystal Ballroom.

At the reception before the planned sit-down dinner, Nadia moved easily among the attendees. Mostly, they were significantly older, so she stood out. The fact that she was alone, and no one knew her, was no obstacle to her ability to engage others in conversation. As a stunning young woman in a red dress, she quickly attracted men who would greet her and introduce themselves.

They would typically engage her in small talk, not expecting a young lady to be conversant in the world's economic issues or the public policy challenges facing the nation. They liked being in her presence but were patronizing toward her.

Olga had made a large donation to the senator's campaign in the name of Mrs. Sinclair. Consequently, the senator's staff was on the lookout for her. Wheeler was the Chairman of the Senate Arms Services Committee so, because of her "late husband's" business, the cyber warfare issue was a topic of interest for her.

At dinner, she was seated at the senator's table, perhaps because of her generous donation level and the hope, by Wheeler's staff, that she might give more. It was a power group at the head table, and, due largely to her intense preparation, she found it easy to converse with the others.

"How prepared is the nation to defend against cyber warfare threats?" she asked Senator Wheeler.

Wheeler smiled unctuously at her and said in his trademark smooth voice, "The NSA has a major department dedicated to the effort, but it is new, and the threat is escalating rapidly. There is a real danger that Internet hackers can bypass the security systems protecting the nation's power grid and financial system and could spy on the country's secret military activities."

As her line of inquiry became more acute, the senator and others at the table were surprised at the depth with which this young woman understood the technical challenges in this critical area.

Nadia only suspected that this dialog might have some relevance to a future mission that Olga had in the planning stages for her. At the table was a younger man, perhaps in his late thirties. He seemed out of place with the big hitters that had been handpicked to sit with the senator.

"Pardon me, I don't think we've been introduced," said Nadia.

He extended his hand; Nadia grasped it warmly. "Richard Davidson. Friends call me Rich. I am a journalist for the *New York Times,* and I have been granted special privileges in covering Senator Wheeler's campaign."

"Elena Sinclair. Pleased to meet you."

"As am I. I would like to know more about your interest in Senator Wheeler. It's awkward to talk here. Would you meet me in the Polo Lounge after the event and submit to an interview?"

Nadia was somewhat reluctant. She did not want to be in a situation where this fellow might probe too deeply. Her training for the Elena Sinclair role had been brief, and she did not want the fallacy of it to be uncovered. Nevertheless, Richard was an attractive young man, and she had little opportunity to interact with men in her general age group. So she relented, but would be careful, very careful.

"I would be pleased to visit with you after the event. But it will need to be a short discussion since I have limited time this evening," she replied.

After the dinner, Senator Wheeler gave the obligatory speech, and the event concluded. She moved on to the Polo Lounge where she met Richard.

Nadia thought that it would deflect his questions if she went on the interrogatory offensive.

"Richard, what is your background, and how did you get such an important journalism assignment?"

Richard told her of his background with some pride. "I attended Yale University and majored in philosophy as an undergrad, then became interested in journalism because it offers great opportunity to think about and inquire into the most important issues of our time and the people behind them.

"I went on to earn my Master's Degree in journalism and was fortunate to be selected as a White House Fellow. As a Fellow, I had the opportunity to serve for a year as an intimate part of the staff for the Secretary of Defense. When I left that public service post at the end of its one-year appointment, my interest in public policy had been piqued. A career in journalism allowed me to pursue that interest."

He smiled ingratiatingly and added, "Mrs. Sinclair, I want to know more about you and your interest in politics. And I'm intrigued by your accent—Eastern European, if I'm not mistaken. Tell me about yourself."

Nadia thought, *The secret to a persuasive untruth is to make it very close to a real truth.*

"I was born in Russia and was educated in mathematics and computer science. When I graduated, opportunities were scarce in my country, and I came to America on a work visa. I signed on with a young, growing Internet security company. The entrepreneur-founder fell in love with me, and soon we were married. As you may have been told, the company was sold about a year ago. Then, recently, my husband died in an automobile accident."

"So that is probably why you are interested in the cyber warfare issue?"

"Correct."

"It must be difficult to lose your husband at such a young age," Richard said with genuine compassion.

"Yes. This last year has been difficult. I have no family here. My husband was very reclusive, so we did not have friends. It has been lonely."

Richard reached across the table and grasped Nadia's hand. "I am sorry. I understand how difficult it must be."

His empathy for "Ms. Sinclair" seemed sincere; it was a male attribute Nadia had rarely observed.

"The senator is only here for another two days, and then I must move on with him," he explained. "But I would like to see you again. Would you join me for dinner tomorrow?"

Nadia continued to be concerned about Richard probing into her fictitious character. He might get suspicious. However, she found him attractive and wanted to spend more time with him. She decided to take the chance.

"Perhaps, but you cannot come to my place," Nadia said hesitantly. "Since my husband's passing, I have lived a very private life and prefer that neighbors not see a gentleman call on me at my home for a while more."

"I understand. The senator, his staff, and I are staying at the Four Seasons Hotel on Doheny Drive. Would you meet me there?"

"Of course. That will be fine. Perhaps eight o'clock would be a suitable time?"

"That works for me. I am delighted. I will meet you there," he confirmed.

"Richard, it has been good to get to know you a little, but it has been a long day for me, and I am tired. I must say good night."

"I want to know more about you—and that's not just my journalistic instinct talking," Richard said. "We will have more time tomorrow evening. Good night, and sleep well."

With that, she walked to the hotel entrance where her car and driver were waiting. Her chauffer seated her, and then drove away.

At the Four Seasons restaurant the next evening, she arrived in her seductive black silk dress. She had only worn that dress when she had "business intentions" but tonight was different. She thought that there might be a romantic interest behind Richard's invitation.

At the senator's fundraiser she had been dressed somewhat formal, in a way that did not reveal the sexy shape of her body. Richard looked at her, stunned at how beautiful she looked

"You look fabulous!" he remarked, holding her chair for her.

"You are too kind," she replied.

He had arranged for an intimate table off in a corner, out of the mainstream of the restaurant.

As the dinner progressed they engaged in a wide-ranging conversation that caused each of them to grow in their respect for each other's perspective. Richard was surprised at the clarity of Nadia's thinking and her grasp of the issues. It was an unexpected pleasure to be able to intellectually engage such a young woman on complex societal and political matters. He was accustomed to spirited discussion at this level with well-informed members of Congress, Ivy League intellectuals, and top professional journalists. This engagement with Elena Sinclair was an enigma to him.

He wondered, *How could this young woman with only an undergraduate degree from a lowly state university argue the issues so intelligently?*

"Richard, what interests you about politics?" Nadia asked, taking a sip of a Kistler Chardonnay that he had selected for her.

"It gives me an opportunity to investigate and analyze matters of public policy," he said.

Nadia nodded pensively. "I find that interesting. You seem like an intelligent man. Politicians, in my opinion, seem like self-interested individuals that only pontificate about issues that are politically popular. They have little understanding of the real challenges facing the world and are only concerned about their re-election. Why do you like hanging around with them?"

"The leaders in Congress are trying to implement policies that help advance our nation and its people," he said defensively. "Not all of them, maybe, but most of them. Or so I'd like to believe. I've tried hard not to become a typically cynical journalist."

"I think you are naïve," Nadia said skeptically. "They have no motivation to pursue initiatives that are in the long-term interest of the nation; nor do they have the wisdom to do it. They promote issues that will get them votes in the next election. I do not find that becoming of a servant of the people."

She continued, "Why don't you investigate and write about some of the serious problems and suffering that goes on around the world? That would be a far more constructive use of your talent."

"I enjoy my interaction with political leaders," Richard said, growing a little irritated with Nadia's viewpoint. "Let's not spoil our evening by arguing over my journalism pursuits. Let's talk about something else."

Their dialogue shifted to the interpersonal dynamics between men and women. It started philosophically, but then turned to a deeper discussion of views about people and relationships. Richard began to understand that this lady had little experience with matters of the heart. This was refreshing compared to the other women—most of them living in the fast lane—that he had known. Elena Sinclair was beautiful and intelligent, Richard thought, but a very alluring aspect of her was her romantic naiveté.

As the conversation lengthened, Nadia was impressed with the philosophic sophistication of Richard's views and his understanding of complex issues, though she was not persuaded on his politics. She was also beginning to realize that he had a genuine appreciation for women and empathy for her and her situation. This was a very unusual man, one of high character and intellect. This appealed to her greatly and increased her sexual attraction to him.

A sense came over her that she might want to move closer to him romantically … and, perhaps, open the door to the possibility of a love relationship. He was young, handsome, intelligent, and seemed to be a person of high principles … although he did seem a little idealistic.

In the bar area, a small combo began to play romantic music. Their first selection was "When I Fall in Love."

"Oh, I love this song,"

"Would you like to dance?" Richard asked.

"That would be … wonderful!" she replied.

Richard was not a highly skilled dancer, but neither was he awkward. He had a good sense of the music. Nadia enjoyed being held in the arms of this attractive, sexy young man. Richard also enjoyed the physical contact with Nadia's fabulous body. He could not help thinking how appealing it was to hold a woman with such a small waist and flat tummy. On Wheeler's campaign trail, he often, out of courtesy, had to dance with older women that were a little, or a lot, more "generous" through their middle. This was real pleasure. She rested her head on his shoulder, and they danced closely.

For Nadia, this was unfamiliar territory. Yet it was an unexpectedly pleasant experience to be held affectionately, romantically, by a man. This was in stark contrast to the animal lust that she always felt from others.

As the evening came to an end, he walked her to the hotel entrance, where her car and driver were again waiting.

"I will be traveling a lot, but hope I can see you again. May I contact you?" Richard said as the driver opened the door to her car.

"I would love it, but for me to maintain my privacy, we will need to communicate solely via e-mail."

"I understand," he responded. "Perhaps we can meet again when our travel schedules permit?"

"That would be wonderful. I look forward to it," she said, knowing that it would be virtually impossible.

For Nadia, there was a problem. Her identity was a fabrication. She was not the widow, Elena Sinclair. If Richard found out that it was a charade, that she had misled him, he would be rightfully upset and probably drop her. If he *really* knew about her nefarious life, there was no way that a relationship could be viable. This was the great dilemma that would trouble her on many occasions in her future.

After being confined to domestic isolation in Russia and likewise in her American marriage, life had finally opened up to her, courtesy of Olga taking her under her wing. Nadia was becoming more of a free spirit, had come to enjoy adventure … and wanted to experience all that the world and life could offer. She had a voracious appetite to taste a wide spectrum of experiences during her time on this planet.

She wondered, *Would a romantic love relationship enhance my life or hold me back?* For her, a real, enduring love relationship might not have a place in her life. At times this saddened her.

The next morning as she lay in bed, she could not get Richard out of her mind. She did not want to let go of him. Her only way forward was to confess about the identity charade.

It was early, but Nadia called Richard's hotel, and the operator connected her to his room.

"Richard, good morning," she said cheerily. "I'm sorry to call so early, but I wanted to reach you before you leave today."

"No problem!" Richard replied. "I have been thinking about you every moment since last night."

"I need to talk to you. Can we meet for breakfast?"

"Of course. My plane doesn't leave until noon."

"I'll be right over and meet you in the restaurant in thirty minutes."

"Done. See you there."

When Nadia arrived, Richard was already there. He had found a nice table that offered a little privacy. As she approached he rose and greeted her.

"I am so glad to see you," he said. "But what is on your mind that is so urgent?"

Nadia was seated. "Well, Richard," she began. "I have a confession to make and did not want you to leave before we talked."

"A confession?"

"Yes. You see, I am not who you think I am."

"What do you mean?"

"There is no Elena Sinclair. My real name is Nadia Borodin."

"Borodin … like the great Russian composer?"

"Yes, and I work for the *Beverly Hills Event Management Company* that put on the evening at the Beverly Hills Hotel for Senator Wheeler. My employer wished to give an anonymous contribution to Senator Wheeler's campaign, but wanted some feedback from the LA event. I was asked to assume Mrs. Sinclair identity and attend that evening.

"I had been reluctant to disclose this to you when we were together, because I did not wish to compromise my employer's effort. And I did not know you. But I would like to continue our relationship and realize that I must set the record straight if we are to continue. I hope you can forgive me this small indiscretion."

"I can accept that, but who the hell are you then?"

Nadia pondered her situation. How much could she tell him without turning him off? The nefarious aspect of her life as an Olga agent would clearly be the end of their relationship, so she took the uncourageous route of not revealing that part of her.

"Much of what I told you was, in fact, true," Nadia explained, somewhat embarrassed for leading him astray. "I came to America on a student visa to attend graduate school. But I ran out of money and had to get a job. Olga, the lady that owns the event management company, took me in, and I work there now."

"The part about you being Russian, was that true?"

"Yes, but I did not tell you that I had a difficult early life. I lived in an orphanage from the time I was an infant, worked my way through college and managed to find my way here."

"That's pretty incredible. Now I'm even more intrigued to know more about you."

Richard had some phone calls to make and had to get to the airport, so he was running out of time.

"I know this must seem presumptuous, since we have only just met, but I do not want this opportunity to slip away. Senator Wheeler and his entourage are moving on to San Francisco for a few days. After our fundraiser activities in the city, I have the weekend off and was planning a visit to Napa Valley. Would you consider joining me there?"

"We must grab these moments when they come to us. So the answer is yes. I will do it."

"Senator Wheeler has many friends and connections, as you know. He has offered me a special place in the valley. From what he has told me, I think we will enjoy it."

"What did he offer?"

Richard smiled inscrutably. "I want it to be a surprise."

So the arrangements were made for their weekend getaway. Nadia was looking forward to this. She had never been with an attractive man for a romantic interlude.

Richard met Nadia at the Oakland Airport, and they drove up to Napa Valley on a Friday afternoon. It was a little more than an hour's drive north from the airport, across the Vallejo bridge, up Route 29 passing through Yountville, to the small town of St. Helena. As they drove up Route 29, Nadia's eyes scanned the beautiful terrain of rolling hills and vineyards. She didn't talk much and seemed pensive.

"You are very quiet, Nadia. Is there something on your mind?" Richard remarked.

"I wonder sometimes where my life is headed," she responded. "You wouldn't know, but my life has been a struggle. I had no parents and spent all of my early life in an orphanage. Now, I find myself in this beautiful place with you."

"I can't imagine what your youth must have been like. I have been fortunate to be born into affluence and have a loving, supportive family. I have not had to struggle at any point. There has been no 'friction' in my life. It has been one that, in many ways, has been unchallenged."

Nadia looked away, out the window again.

"It's difficult for me to know how to relate to someone coming from your background," she said.

Richard smiled. "Don't try. Just be yourself. I am excited about the adventure in our relationship. I have never known anyone like you. All the women in my life attended private schools, went to Ivy League universities, joined sororities, and were supported by affluent parents. They are all perfectly groomed and very proper. There is a boring sameness about all of them."

This was an interesting perspective coming from him. Nadia had thought that their disparate backgrounds would make it difficult for the two of them to relate, but it seemed, to the contrary, their differences *were* the appeal. Each shared a curiosity about the other and a desire to explore the unknown corners of that other person who had walked a different road in life. That was the magic of the attraction.

They soon arrived in St. Helena, turned left, and headed west for a few blocks. At the dead end of the street they arrived at the entrance to a large estate. Richard stopped the car in front of the entry gates.

"Is this where we are staying?" Nadia asked.

"This is it."

Nadia opened the car door and jumped out to look at the visual feast before her. There was a very tall hedge, over ten feet high that bordered the street and a large European-style iron gate at the entrance to the property. On the gate, in an arc across it, was the name of the estate: *Spottswoode*. Looking through the gate she could see a large Victorian house and huge trees on the grounds. A graveled circular driveway led to the front of the house. This was obviously a very old estate.

"Richard, what do you know about this place?" Nadia asked.

Richard explained that the classic Victorian house was built in 1882. It was purchased by Mary Novak and her now deceased husband in 1972 and had been owned and developed by her ever since.

"Their vineyards are behind the residence," he said.

He rang the house and a worker came to the gate and let them in. He directed them to a secluded guest house on the north end of the estate. As they approached it they passed a beautiful black-bottomed pool. The guest house was a private two-story home that looked out on the vineyard. Flushed with anticipation, they moved in and got settled.

"This is fabulous!" Nadia remarked.

Richard grinned appreciatively. "I am going to owe Wheeler some great press for this."

On a coffee table Nadia noticed a big fat guest log that looked very old. She sat down and began paging through it.

"Look at all the people that have stayed here! Here's a note from Julia Child back in the 1980s. She wrote parts of one of her books here."

"I'm going up to the bedroom to shower and change for dinner," Richard said, heading up the stairs. "You can come up when you're finished looking at the book. It's been a long day for me, so let's do an early dinner."

Nadia was fascinated with the history of Spottswoode and wanted to spend more time looking at the guest log book.

"That is fine with me. I'll be up in a minute."

They dressed for dinner.

"A friend recommended an Italian restaurant named Tra Vigne in town," Richard commented. "I made a reservation for us, and I thought it would be nice to walk there. It's not far."

"Sounds delightful," said Nadia, tidying up his Windsor knot. "I'm ready."

He took her hand as they left to walk to the restaurant. Swinging her around and looking at her in an admiring way, he said, "You look gorgeous!"

Nadia smiled and thought, *Perhaps this will be a pleasant few days with this attractive man.*

Richard then pulled her close, embraced her, and kissed her passionately. A warm glow settled across her and she felt aroused.

"Wow! That was unexpected," she exclaimed.

Richard shrugged with boyish charm. "Your beauty overcame me, and I could not help myself."

"For a kiss like that, I'm always available."

They took the short walk of eight blocks or so to the restaurant and were seated for dinner.

"I love Italian food," Nadia said.

"Good," Richard replied. "I hope you brought your appetite. My friend said the food here is to die for."

A waiter approached their table. "Would you like to order some wine?" he asked.

"Of course!" Richard said. "Do you have anything new that I might not know?"

"Ed Sbragia, the winemaker emeritus from Beringer, has been making his own wines in recent years. He makes a great Chardonnay, but is best known for his cabs. We have his Howell Mountain Cabernet Sauvignon that I can offer you."

"Excellent. We will try it."

Richard and Nadia enjoyed a wonderful dinner, and the wine tuned out to be a pleasant surprise.

"Have you ever been married?" Richard asked.

"Yes, it was my pathway to citizenship. But there was no romance in it, and it didn't last.

"How about you?"

"I guess I haven't met the right girl. I have been working hard and traveling a lot, so it's been difficult to develop a lasting relationship."

"This is purely a rhetorical question," Nadia began tentatively, "but could you ever have an interest in … someone like me?"

Richard smiled and took a sip of the cabernet. "I have never been around someone like you. It's an intriguing thing to think about. Up to now the women in my life have had nothing to add to me. You come from a different world … not just geographically, but in the full spectrum of how you have lived life. I must say, there is a certain appeal to developing a connection with you."

Nadia frowned. "A connection? *That's* romantic."

"Sorry. I meant that perhaps, at some point, I could really fall for you."

"Don't play with me, Richard! A journey into love would take me across a new frontier. I am naïve about such things and could easily be hurt."

"Nadia, you were the one that raised the question. I only answered you … honestly. But you should know that one cannot venture into love without taking risks."

"I don't know if I could go there. I'm not good with that affection stuff."

Richard's response was slow and measured. "Someday you will have to let yourself go."

Nadia found herself conflicted. She was attracted to Richard and speculated about the possibly of a love relationship with him. It was an exciting thought, something she had not yet experienced. But this was just a weekend fling, where they were in the early stages of getting to know each other. *Were there real possibilities for them, beyond this brief encounter?* In a way it was less important to know, because she was unsure herself how much she might want out of the relationship. *So*, she thought, *I'm getting way ahead of myself. Let's take one step forward at a time and see where it leads.*

Back in their room, they were retiring. Richard was the first to go to bed while Nadia finished up a woman's normal preparations before turning in for the night. Nadia liked to sleep in a simple T-shirt and nothing else. When she returned to their bedroom, Richard had fallen asleep. Nadia thought, *What a bummer. I know he was tired after his long day. I'll get him in the morning.*

It did not take that long. A little before daybreak Richard rolled over and came in contact with her, arousing her out of her sleep. He did not wear pajamas, and his warm body snuggled up against hers. He embraced her instinctively although initially he was only half awake.

It was dark in the room, but a sliver of moonlight through a window outlined his profile against the darkness. She ran her hands across the muscular terrain of his body. *I like this,* she thought. Richard had a trim physique with no hair on his chest, his biceps, or back, making it easy for her hand to glide across it. She loved touching him. He slid down, pressing his face into her breasts and kissed them with erotic abandon. His warm hands roved all over her with passion.

She grasped his head and pulled it tighter into her breasts, then pushed it lower into her abdomen. His tongue slid across her very sensitive groin area. Her desire for him was raging. She ran her fingernails across his back, wanting to scratch him hard, but did it with restraint.

She lay on her back with him over her. In the dim light, she could just barely make out the image of him over her, but she had a keen sense of him. She wanted to feel his passion and wrapped her hand around his erect and very hard member. She paused for a moment, enjoying the sensation and feeling the blood pulsating through it.

Nadia said jokingly to him, "I know what to do with this thing. I know how to make it happy."

"I am yours to do with what you like," he moaned.

She guided it into her waiting pleasure zone, and a surge of excitement engulfed them.

In a brief moment, she thought about Alexandra and the pleasures she had confessed. *This* was what lovemaking is about.

In the morning, as warm sun rays streamed through the windows of the cottage, they lay in bed touching and talking, enjoying the moment.

"Nadia, at times, you have seemed guarded with me, as if you have some dark secret … something I should know about you."

"Richard, please don't probe. Some things are better left alone."

"Okay, but if we go further, I will want to know everything."

The weekend continued with long walks, tours of wineries, and many long, stimulating conversations. Also, the sex was outstanding, and they often sneaked back to the cottage at Spottswoode to continue their more primal engagement. But sadly, the weekend passed quickly. Richard needed to catch a Sunday flight to the East Coast, and Nadia suspected that something was up with Olga, so it was time for her to get back to LA.

At the San Francisco Airport they were saying their goodbyes.

"Richard, I loved our weekend together."

"Nadia, remember what I said about opening yourself up to love. You are a fascinating woman and have a lot to offer a man … perhaps me."

"Richard, we come from two very different worlds. It would be a challenge for both of us. There may be no place for us in this crazy world. And anyway, you know that I have difficulty dealing with affection."

"Nadia, you can break out of the emotional trap of your childhood. Give love a chance."

"Perhaps. Maybe we can connect again?"

"I would like that very much. Let's stay in touch. I will be traveling a lot, but you have my e-mail, and I have yours."

Then, just before they parted, Richard pulled her to him again and kissed her passionately.

On the plane ride back to LA, Nadia reflected on their weekend. It had been wonderful for her to experience a romantic moment in her life. Her dilemma remained that she was engaged in a "line of work" that Richard, or any man, would find objectionable. This would present a challenge to the prospect of any serious relationship. Still, the door was now open, and the fire of romantic love was beginning to burn in her.

Back at the Malibu house Olga was sitting alone in her study, reading. Alexandra approached her.

"Olga, how is my friend Nadia doing?"

"She is doing surprisingly well," Olga said. "Why don't you have a seat and let's talk."

"I am a little concerned about her," Alexandra began. "She has achieved a great deal of success on the first two assignments that you gave her. I must say that I am impressed, since she has been with us for such a short period. However, she seems like a lost soul when it comes to romance."

"While Nadia is an exceptionally bright young woman, she is still immature emotionally," Olga remarked. "One can appreciate that, understanding the lack of affection that she experienced in her young life. She likes you, Alexandra. You can help her develop in matters of love. Its one reason that I matched you up with her. Even beginning to connect emotionally with affection, would be good for her."

"I also have grown quite fond of her," Alexandra admitted. "I will do what I can, but she is so bright it's hard for me to keep up with her at times."

Olga smiled. "Alex, I know a lot more about her than you may think, perhaps even more than she knows about herself. Nadia is truly gifted, so gifted that it is unlikely that you or I will ever know anyone even close to her level of intelligence. But, a superior mind is only part of what makes up a whole person, and she needs to develop emotionally, more fully as an individual. You can help her with that. I am confident that it will come, but she has a long way to travel to realize her full potential as a human being. We are her family now and should help her as much as we can."

"What motivates her?" Alexandra asked. "She now has enough money to live comfortably. I don't want her to leave us."

Olga grew pensive. "I have known a number of individuals that function at a stratospheric level … but none quite as superior as she. Once their struggle for survival and basic needs for economic security are met, a higher tier of motivations sets in. These may not be easy for you and me to relate to, but for someone like Nadia, it is what drives her.

"Nadia has a voracious intellectual appetite for challenge. It is like a demon that lives in her brain—in that beautiful mind—and *it must be fed*. She must see action that tests her limits. So, in a way, it is *the game*, not the reward, that motivates her.

"Nadia is a very unique creature. I am fascinated by her extraordinary intelligence and the kind of person that it creates. It is my objective to keep her challenged and thrilled with what she is doing. In her next assignment, I will be stepping up the complexity of the challenge she faces. She will need to raise her game to complete it successfully."

"Do you think she can do it?" Alexandra asked.

Olga smiled inscrutably. "We shall see, my child, we shall see."

# CHAPTER 9

# CAP D'ANTIBES

IT HAD COME TIME FOR NADIA'S next assignment. It was a late day in March when Olga asked Nadia to meet her in the drawing room at the Malibu house to talk about her next mission. The drawing room was also a library and contained a rich collection of great books. With its massive stone fireplace and bay window overlooking the Pacific, it was, not surprisingly, Nadia's favorite room in the house. She loved to go prowling through the bookshelves looking for wonderful things to read. She would often go there by herself during her quiet time away from the busy activities of Olga's enterprise.

Nadia arrived at the drawing room a little before Olga and began browsing through the books, as she had many times before. She pulled out a well-worn copy of Leo Tolstoy's *Anna Karenina*, a novel that she loved. She put it back in its place, let her fingertip glide across the shelf, and spotted a book by Alexander Pushkin, Russia's most famous poet. She pulled it out and browsed through the pages, stopping for a moment to read a few verses from "Morpheus."

It was dusk and the sun was setting, but it would be an hour or so before dinner was served. At long last, Olga arrived.

"Sorry to have kept you waiting," she said. "Would you like a glass of sherry?"

"That would be splendid," Nadia responded, knowing that something was up. The drawing room was the venue that Olga typically selected when she was ready to make an assignment.

"Do you have a new adventure for me?" Nadia said, anticipating Olga's next move.

Olga eyed her critically. "You seem anxious. Perhaps things are moving too slow for you lately."

"Perhaps so," Nadia said. "What do you have in mind for me?"

"Your next assignment is the most challenging that we have yet considered for you … and potentially the most dangerous that any of my agents have pursued," Olga warned, beginning her orientation.

"In the south of France, particularly in the Antibes region of the Cote d'Azur, Russian oligarchs have been buying up the prime Mediterranean sea-front properties. Nadia, you have no idea how much wealth these Russian men have amassed in a very short time through the privatization of Soviet industries. They are building the biggest yachts in the world; three under construction are over 500 feet in length. One mini-oligarch recently was divorced after two years of marriage. His wife received £220 million—about 360 million American dollars—in the settlement.

"This looks like a target rich area," she explained, "but it is dangerous. These men can be ruthless and do not fear the authorities. If you are interested, I will relocate you there and set you up. I have connections in the area that can be helpful in the pursuit of your mission."

"I do not like Russian men!" Nadia said emphatically. "They have no respect for women and treat them badly. I have personally been abused by them for too many years."

Olga smiled impishly. "Then it should give you some pleasure to pull off a big sting on one of them!"

"Perhaps, but this promises to be a very distasteful experience … an unpleasant duty. The danger does not trouble me. How much can we make on this idea?" Nadia asked.

"It's hard to say, but there is essentially no limit. At the end we hope to get you out alive, with no traceability to your identity." Olga searched Nadia's face; she could see she was not dissuaded by the risk and, perhaps, intrigued by the adventure the mission promised. "Of course, if you have misgivings, you do not have to take this assignment. You have over $20 million in your Swiss bank account, and there are other less dangerous, less challenging missions that you can pursue."

Without hesitation Nadia responded, "I do not have to think about it. I do not have a life outside of *the agency* and I am enthusiastic about any mission that you might propose. I'm thrilled to take on the next assignment—especially if it gives me a chance to give some grief to a Russian man."

"I like your attitude," Olga said. "We will need a few weeks to prepare for this mission, so you may relax for a while."

"I am tired of this blonde hair," Nadia said. "I would like to go back to my natural brunette color. Do you have any problem with that?"

"Actually that's a good idea. It will better suit your next mission," Olga responded.

About a week later, Olga called Nadia back to the drawing room.

"There is a change to the plan. I was contacted by my 'old employer,' and they have asked for my help. There is a developing threat that they are in the early stages of fleshing out. It involves a possible cyber-attack on the United States. I have helped them out before, and they occasionally call on me because of my unconventional and effective means. In return, they have offered protection and information reciprocity at times.

"There are sometimes certain aspects of a mission that cannot be done by their staff," Olga continued. "On those occasions, my agency serves as an outsource contractor. My former employer, for example, could not hire you for a deep classified mission, particularly if it required a crypto-class, top-secret security clearance. Your Russian heritage and somewhat dubious past would rule you out. Also, you can do things that no government employee could be asked to do. Yet you are the perfect instrument for the project. Your

Russian heritage and knowledge of computer sciences are critical for this assignment."

"You will need to undergo an intensive training program in cyber technology, especially as it relates to electronic funds transfer and Internet commerce. This phase of your special education will take about three to four months. I also want you to take part of that time to get acquainted with some of my other *agents* and meet some of the new girls that I have recruited into *the agency*.

"My 'former employer' has advised me that this is a matter of the highest national priority. They fear that the cyber technology being developed could threaten the security of the US financial system. Coincidently, the intelligence operations of the US government believe that a Russian oligarch, perhaps backed by a government agency, is planning a first attack to validate the effectiveness of the cyber systems that they are developing.

"So it fits into our plan also. They have traced some of the failed attacks to an area in the south of France or Mediterranean Sea region. I already have our operations center working on the research element, and a field agent in the Cote d' Azure area is beginning advanced work on the project. You will need to be ready by summer."

*Has Olga really retired from the CIA*, Nadia wondered, *or has she set up a special, clandestine field operation that just looks like a private enterprise? Her relationship with her "old employer" seems to be much closer than that of a retiree.* Nadia was curious about Olga's relationship to her "old employer" but dared not ask, and it would remain a mystery to her.

"Your assignment will be to infiltrate the oligarch's technical team and seek to neutralize the threat," Olga said. "This is even more dangerous than I first indicated to you. Again, you do not have to do this, but you are the best equipped agent in my organization to attempt this complex mission."

"I will do it!" Nadia said with a certain conviction.

Back at the office for the *Beverly Hills Event Management Company*,

Nadia made her first visit to the basement, where the operations center was located. Mark Ainsworth, the operations center manager, gave her the tour. She was amazed at what she saw. There was a highly sophisticated operation working behind the scenes to support Olga's field agents.

The room was dimly lit, but the cool glow from computer screens added an almost sinister ambience to the place. There was a large screen that depicted a map of the globe and a number of blown-up sections showing details of selected cities. Nadia noticed color-coded markers on the screen that were replicated on workstations in various locations around the room.

She asked the operations manager about the markers. "Those are our field agents," Mark explained. "All agents have a subcutaneous GPS microchip implanted on them so we can track them at all times. You have one too. One night, soon after you joined *the agency*, we sedated you while you were asleep and completed the procedure. It is for your own security and so our staff can support you effectively. The red markers are the agents themselves and the green markers are our field security backup staff."

Nadia was upset that Olga had inserted the GPS tracking chip in her without her permission. "I wish Olga had asked me before doing it."

"You have a right to be upset," Mark Ainsworth said. "But Olga insists that it be done to every agent. She is obsessively concerned about the safety of her girls."

He continued, "Each work station is for a field agent and is monitored by the operations staff 24/7. We cannot afford any mistakes or any breaches of security. We have never lost an agent or had one compromised."

Escorting her to one of the workstations, Mark said, "Nadia, I would like you to meet Anna, the liaison officer that is in charge of your mission support functions."

Anna appeared to be in her mid-forties. She had been a field agent for a while when she was younger, but was not cut out for it. She had too much empathy for the targets. Also, she was now married and was living in the West LA area. This was her full-time job, and she was good at it. Nadia was delighted to get to know Anna. Mark told her that her identity needed to remain confidential, but Nadia could access Anna whenever she wanted. When on field assignments she would refer to Anna as "liaison officer 307."

"Please report down here at seven tomorrow morning, and we will get started," Mark told Nadia.

As Nadia drove back to Olga's house in Malibu she thought, I *have no privacy! Olga knows my every move.* This was uncomfortable for her, but it was also good to know the intensity with which *the agency* was watching out for her in potentially risky situations.

The next morning Nadia reported to the Operations Center promptly at 7:00 am. Mark laid out the plan.

"Nadia, we will be providing you with a great deal of the information that you need to carry out your next mission. However, because of the critical nature of it and the technical aspects of the mission, we have also arranged for you to receive input from external sources that have an interest in your success.

"I have arranged a travel itinerary for you, commencing next week. You will receive high-level briefings from three government agencies. Access to the activities and methods of these agencies are generally not available to a private individual, but through Olga's connections and the influence of Senator Wheeler, doors have been opened for you. While you will not have access to confidential information at these organizations, there is much you can learn that will be helpful to you when you pursue your mission.

"Your first stop will be at the National Security Agency in Fort Meade, Maryland. The NSA is responsible for hacking into foreign information systems and monitoring foreign communications of all types in order to advise American policy makers and leaders in the Executive Branch of government on international activities that might be adverse to our nation's interests. This is an organization with exceptional technical talent, with deep expertise in cryptography and other essential disciplines."

Nadia remembered Senator Wheeler's comments about a newly formed division within the NSA that focused on cyber warfare. On this trip, she would learn that the new organization, formed in May 2010, was the US Cyber Command (USCYBERCOM). She would be briefed by their technical staff.

"The second stop on your information gathering tour will be at the CIA Headquarters in McLean, Virginia," Mark went on. "There you will meet with staff members of the National Clandestine Service that conducts covert action in dangerous venues around the world. Obviously, there is much that they cannot tell you, but learn what you can.

"Lastly, you will visit the US Treasury Department in Washington. You will meet with the Technical Operations Division and learn about the electronic funds transfer systems in the United States and the firewalls that protect electronic financial transactions from nefarious intruders. Without a security clearance or need-to-know status, you will not be exposed to the particulars of how the systems and security measures are implemented. However, these briefings will educate you on the general character of the infrastructure of these systems. It is all you need to know to conduct your mission."

Nadia spent a month on the road learning as much as she could. Those providing the briefings were astonished at how well she grasped the technical aspects of their activities. The briefings at NSA would turn out to be the most valuable. It was there that she learned from high-level experts about computer "worms": sets of computer code that can be implanted into computer and communications systems. Once inside they can spy on the activities going on in the computers and gather critical information. More sophisticated ones are capable of taking malicious action on the host that they have invaded.

Perhaps the most infamous recent example was the worms that caused the centrifuges in Iran's uranium enrichment facility to go haywire, spinning out of control and self-destructing. It was an international incident of epic proportions. Most suspected the CIA or Israeli Special Forces, but perhaps no one will ever know who hacked into the Iranian system and planted the worms.

On her return from Washington, Nadia took a detour to the San Francisco Bay area and visited some of the top networking and communications companies. She met the Internet-hacking "geeks" (a term used endearingly and derogatorily at the same time) that were trying to devise methods for breaking into large government and private systems. This was necessary for the technical staff to build the security systems to protect them. All this was fascinating to Nadia, and the knowledge she acquired on their techniques would prove invaluable as her mission unfolded. At every agency and tech company, the mostly male staffs were amazed at how quickly and thoroughly Nadia grasped the complexities of their work. *This must be a very bright young woman*, they thought.

The months flew by quickly, and it was now spring and time to mobilize Nadia. She had gone through extensive training in cyber insurgency methods, the global and US technologies for the electronic transfer of funds, modern cryptographic schemes and algorithms, and a comprehensive briefing on electronic commerce. She had learned about the Automated Clearing House (ACH), an electronic network that is the backbone for financial transactions in the United States. The ACH processes funds transfers for the Federal Reserve Banks, commercial banks, and a huge volume of online consumer deposits and payments. Each year it handles over $100 trillion in fund transfers.

The NSA had reason to believe that the electronic funds transfer system was being targeted by an obscure cyber initiative based somewhere in the South of France. This was not a terrorist organization; it was a private enterprise focused on extracting a great deal of money from the system. They suspected that a Russian oligarch was behind it, but did not know for sure.

Nadia's mission was to go there and attempt to destroy the threat.

"What do we get if we succeed in this mission?" she asked Olga. "We are not a public service organization."

"They will pay all our expenses and give us a $25 million success fee, if we can pull it off," Olga responded.

"That's not very much for a mission of this complexity and danger," Nadia responded.

"True, but where is your patriotic spirit?" Olga said. "This is in the national interest. In addition to neutralizing the national security threat, we may be able to extract a prize out of the perpetrator."

Nadia was intrigued. "That is a fascinating opportunity to think about!"

Nadia relocated to the south of France, not really certain where all this would lead. She found an apartment in the small seaside town of Juan les Pins adjacent to Antibes. Anna, in the operations center, told her to expect a call from an Andre Popov, who had been conducting field research and investigative work for the CIA on this mission. He would brief her on the latest information related to her assignment.

Popov thought that his identity was completely secure, but did not want to take any chances, so the meeting took place at her apartment.

"We believe that the man behind the cyber threat is Vladimir Russoff," said Popov, getting down to business. "He is one of the top oligarchs, as well as one of the wealthiest men in Russia. He owns a large industrial company and is a defense contractor. Russoff's father was an influential member of the Soviet Politburo.

"After the dissolution of the Soviet Union, the leadership of Russia pursued an aggressive privatization of the government-owned enterprises. Because of his father's political position and influence, the senior Mr. Russoff was able to guide these two large companies into his son's hands. Vladimir continues to have deep connections in the Russian military, the secret police, and the government leadership. We do not know the extent of those relationships but suspect that he is working closely with them. He is an educated man, having graduated from the London School of Business, but also a man to be feared. We must be careful.

"Communiqués that we have intercepted indicate that he has been lent a small team of cyber techies from the Federal Security Service of the Russian Federation. The FSB is the principal successor to the KGB. That bureau is in charge of counter-intelligence, surveillance, counter-terrorism, and internal and border security. It also includes a sophisticated cyber warfare operation.

"We have not been able to confirm the existence of this cyber insurgency team or where it is located," Popov went on. "However, the NSA has reported a series of attempts on the Treasury Department's accounts. Fortunately, they are protected by an industrial-strength firewall and transactions involve high-tech cryptography methods that we believe to be virtually infallible. Our nation cannot take this security for granted. These insurgents are becoming increasingly sophisticated. We need to neutralize this threat before they find a way in."

"I do not mind challenges, but if we do not know where this team is, or even whether it exists, how can I proceed?" Nadia asked.

"We have an idea that might draw them out and get you inside their operation." Popov said. "You are going to be arrested for hacking into a French credit card system and getting caught. You will go to jail. There will be a story in the press that describes you as a highly skilled cyber-criminal who was able to accomplish the virtually impossible task of penetrating a highly fortified system through their vaunted firewall. We have used our 'special means' to make these arrangements.

"We are counting on Russoff's team seeing this story and using his power to bail you out and recruit you to help them. We know that they are constantly searching the Internet for any news of skilled attacks on the financial system. It is virtually certain that they will pick up on the news of your arrest."

"That is a creative strategy, but if it doesn't work, you need to get me out of there!" Nadia insisted.

"Getting you out of the jail would be no problem," Popov assured her. "But, once you are inside Russoff's operation, you will be on your own. It is doubtful that you will even be able to communicate with us."

Nadia was on board with the assignment and anxious to get started. It seemed like a grand adventure to her. "I was warned that this might be a difficult and risky mission, but it's what I signed up for. Let's move ahead."

A few days later Nadia was hauled off to jail by the local police and the story broke in the newspapers. It was a sensational story, receiving front-page attention, that portrayed Nadia as an e-commerce insurgent and computer genius that had found a way to get into the systems of a large French bank.

The article in the *Nice Matin* newspaper read:

## Computer Hacker Jailed on Daring Cyber-attack on French Bank

Nice, France — In the nearby town of Juan les Pins, a young Russian woman has been jailed for a failed attempt to break into the accounts of one of the largest banks in France. In this unprecedented instance of Internet thievery, she sought not to simply steal credit card information, but to actually transfer funds out of the bank to an undisclosed location.

Bank officials refused to disclose how they uncovered the plot or the identity of the young woman, pending the completion of their investigation. It was reported that a special team from the bank's headquarters in Paris was being dispatched to question her to uncover how she was able to get past the extensive firewall systems of the bank. Bank officials were puzzled by how this amateur computer hacker could have come so close to pulling off the heist.

The scheme worked, and the next day two men arrived at the police station and arranged for her release. She suspected that some significant bribe money had changed hands or perhaps some oligarch-style coercion had taken place. The two men guided her to a black van that waited curbside, forced her in, and sped away. They drove down the Cap d'Antibe toward the point of this small peninsula that juts out into the Mediterranean. They turned down a long driveway to a large villa, perched high atop a cliff commanding awe-inspiring vistas of the azure sea.

*This must be Russoff's place*, Nadia thought.

At the entrance, an older gentleman introduced himself as the house manager for Mr. Russoff. He greeted her politely in a French accent and escorted her to a terrace off of the main salon of the house. There she met Vladimir Russoff.

Russoff was an imposing figure of a man, as she had imagined him. He stood six-feet-two and had a large muscular build, probably developed when he served in the Soviet military as a young man. He was now fifty-four, but remained in good physical shape. His hair was dark with a slight graying at the temples and was tightly trimmed in a crew cut. He had a large-featured, masculine face with weathered skin. His hands seemed large even for the size of his body. While not really handsome in a normal sense, there was a ruggedness about him that evoked a primal attraction for Nadia. There was an extreme air of self-confidence about him. He was the image of power and wealth, a man that knew no boundaries to what he could do. Just the image of Russoff would evoke fear in the hearts of those that came in contact with him.

That day Russoff was dressed in a black shirt and trousers and wearing a steel-gray sport coat with no tie. He spoke in a deep resonating voice.

"Please be seated," he said in a surprisingly courteous manner.

A steward arrived and offered her a glass of champagne. The setting was fabulous on this terrace jutting out over a rocky cliff with the blue

Mediterranean shimmering below. There was a large black-hulled motor yacht anchored off the villa's shore, stern-tied to big boulders on the beach below. She had been on the *Invictus*, so she was not new to large yachts, but Russoff's was unusually large.

The Russian flag was flying proudly off its stern. Russoff saw her looking at the yacht.

"I am a lover of classical music, in particular the Russian classics. You can see that the name of my yacht is the *Russian Five*. Do you know the *Russian Five*?" he asked.

"Of course! I have Russian blood in my veins, as do you," said Nadia. "The *Russian Five* were nineteenth century composers, based in Saint Petersburg, dedicated to creating a national school of Russian music that could thrive without the suffocating influence of other Western European forms. Their names were Modest Mussorgsky, Nikolay Rimsky-Korsakov, Aleksandr Borodin, Mily Balakirev, and Cesar Cui."

Russoff was impressed. "You know your history."

"I also love music," she replied.

"I may have a proposition for you, young lady," Russoff said. "You have been reported to have some special skills in the area of electronic funds transfer. There may be a project on which you can be helpful to me. However, it is a very sensitive matter, and I would need to be certain about your commitment to handling all aspects of it with discretion. I am prepared to reward you handsomely for your effort, if you can help me succeed.

"Your attempted 'sting operation' on the French bank tells me that you are, perhaps, willing to take on assignments that might not be entirely legal. Is that so?"

"What do you have in mind?" she asked, evading his question.

"I have a small team that is attempting an Internet-based heist somewhat like what you attempted but much more complex and on a much larger scale," Russoff explained. "Nadia, I need to advise you that I demand absolute loyalty and confidentiality on my projects. I warn you: if you choose to take on this assignment and if you are not trustworthy to perfection … there will be dire consequences. There are no limits to my power and what I can do. You must not compromise the effort in any way!"

"I know the danger I am in. You could send me back to jail. You could make me disappear, since no one knows where I am. My options are limited—"

"Indeed they are!" Russoff interrupted her. "Should you choose to accept, you will have talented help on the assignment that I have for you … but you had better not fail or breach the confidentiality of the project."

He continued. "If you agree, my men will take you to the site where the project work is going on. You will be briefed there on your assignment."

Nadia cocked her head and said impudently, "So, what's in it for me?"

"I will pay you 10,000 euros per month and a large bonus if you are successful," Russoff said. "I will let you know the amount of the bonus later, after your contribution to the effort is clear."

"That is good enough for now. I'll do it!"

"There is one more thing," Russoff said, "I am a very careful man on such matters and will need a few days to check you out. You will stay here in one of my guest rooms, under our 'protection' while we are doing our due diligence on you."

Nadia's apprehension rose. She thought, *God, I hope Olga's operations center has done a bulletproof job on the makeover of my background. If there is any flaw that might be detected, I could be in trouble.*

Russoff's men completed their background investigations, and it all checked out. Olga's operations center team and the CIA had collaborated to plant or create files and records of an official nature that provided proof of Nadia's past.

According to the fabricated story, she had escaped from Russia and moved to Paris, where she met and married an American executive, Thomas Barksdale, who was based there. When her husband was abducted by a terrorist group seeking ransom money, the United States government declined to pay for his release. He was killed and she became bitter toward the American government. She had a French passport, but it showed her place of birth to be a suburb of Moscow, not Bryansk. Also, her Russian last name had been changed, and the last name on her passport was that of the American executive that she had married in Paris. The records showed that she had graduated from a state university with a degree in computer science.

While she lived in Paris she had a job in the IT department of Banco Paribas, one of the world's largest banks. She worked for several years as part of the group that developed software systems to support the bank's global electronic funds transfer operations.

To Russoff this was a perfect fit—the missing link in his team that was attempting to devise code to break into the US Treasury Department accounts.

It was the beginning of summer, and Nadia was enjoying a light continental breakfast on a terrace off the dining area of the villa. As the morning sun warmed her skin, Russoff approached her, apparently in a pleasant mood.

"Nadia, we have good news. Our background checks have come back satisfactory, and we can move ahead with your assignment. The project is being conducted in a very private location on the Island of Sardinia, which is part of Italy. I have another place there, and you will like it.

"You will leave tomorrow for Sardinia, but this evening I would like you to join me for dinner. We will be dining out, so please dress appropriately."

Nadia thought, *"Appropriately"—what did that mean?* She decided that it was back to her simple black silk dress. That evening she joined Russoff in the villa's motor court. As they waited for his car and driver, another couple joined them. Russoff introduced them.

"Nadia, I would like you to meet Yuri Petrovski, the Chief Financial Officer of my company, and this is Nina, his friend."

Nina was a very beautiful brunette, much younger than Petrovski. From her accent Nadia thought that she might be Serbian. He made no mention of her as a wife, colleague, or "traveling companion." Russoff and Nadia left in the first car, followed by his CFO, and then a black van that Nadia assumed to be Russoff's security agents.

It was a short trip. Their small motorcade turned down Boulevard John F. Kennedy toward the tip of Cap d'Antibes. Soon they arrived at the Hôtel du Cap-Eden Roc. This, one of the great hotel properties in the world, is located on twenty-two pristine, park-like acres. The main building is a classic nineteenth-century French chateau located a few hundred yards back from the sea. From the main building a large lawn sweeps downhill to the seaside building called Eden Roc. At Eden Roc, there is a saltwater pool, an elegant restaurant, and waterfront cabanas.

*Hotel du Cap at Antibes*

It was there, in this remarkable setting, that they were to dine. Early on, the dinner conversation was simply a social dialogue between the two men. Nadia and the other woman remained silent, except to order their food and drink.

At some point Russoff and the CFO of his industrial company were engaged in a debate on a matter relating to a large contract that the company had been awarded. The contract was to provide heavy machinery to a shipbuilding company in South Korea. The manufacturing was to take place at one of Russoff's plants in Eastern Europe. Accordingly, the costs would be in the euro currency and payment would be made in the South Korean currency, known as won.

*Pool & dining area at Eden Roc*

The issue was whether or not to hedge out the currency risk. Russoff's CFO argued strongly in favor of putting on the hedge, as he did not like the prospect of having currency exposure. Russoff himself was somewhat hesitant. If the euro was to strengthen with respect to the won, their costs would go up verses the revenue, paid in the South Korean currency. This would put the contract into a loss. As the debate progressed, the CFO's lady companion sat quietly eating her dinner.

Then came a point when Nadia hesitantly said, "Gentlemen, may I offer an opinion?"

Russoff's CFO quickly, dismissively, commented that she should keep her thoughts to herself and enjoy her dinner. Nadia was a little annoyed but politely responded.

"With all due respect, Mr. Petrovski, I have worked for a large international bank, and, although I was not in their currency department, in the electronic funds transfer operation I was able to observe quite a lot."

The Russian CFO began to discredit her when Russoff intervened.

"Yuri, humor me for a minute, and let's hear what the lady has to say."

Nadia then laid out a thoughtful case for a directional currency bet. Her macroeconomic argument was that there was a good chance that the euro would decline in value, and the South Korean won would increase in value over the term of the contract. If the company did not hedge out its currency exposure, this could add significantly to the profitability of the deal, albeit adding some risk. Nadia knew that Russoff was an aggressive man that did not shy away from risk. His CFO, like most in such positions, was conservative and always sought to avoid risk.

Russoff delighted in Nadia's ingenious rebuttal but could not help thinking, *Who is this woman? Just working in Banco Paribas was not enough to give her this knowledge about international finance.* Furthermore, he was amazed at the intellectual prowess that she demonstrated in arguing the case. How could all this be coming out of a beautiful young woman, perhaps only in her late twenties?

If he only knew that he was in the presence of an exceptional anomaly of the female species, and she was on a mission to cause him harm.

They finished the dinner in that beautiful setting at Eden Roc, then returned to the villa for the night. Russoff was becoming quite attracted to Nadia, but did not pursue her since she was a critical part of a big "sting" operation that he had underway.

In the morning, Nadia was picked up and taken to the airport at Nice where Russoff's private plane was waiting to fly her to Olbia on the northern coast of Sardinia.

Russoff's Sardinia villa was near Porto Cervo on the Costa Smeralda. A driver would meet her there and take her to the Cala di Volpe hotel where she would stay for the night. Nadia would be picked up the next day and driven to Russoff's villa to begin work. His project team had been notified of her arrival and would brief her on the project the next day.

As her plane approached the landing strip at Olbia, it flew low over the Costa Smeralda. She looked down at the crystal clear emerald-green water and elegant villas that dotted the coastline. She also saw in the harbor a huge number of super yachts. She worried that perhaps Roberto might be here. She looked hard at the yachts below, trying, without success, to spot the *Invictus*. Although she had changed her hair color and cut, there was a possibility that he would recognize her. She would need to be careful.

The Cala di Volpe is the premier hotel in the very exclusive Costa Smeralda area. It is a retreat for wealthy Italians, other Europeans of means, and global travelers at the highest level. It is a pick-up and drop-off destination for guests boarding or disembarking from large yachts cruising the waters in this area.

When she checked into the Cala di Volpe, she asked if they had a guest by the name of Roberto Bartolini.

The reception clerk smiled in recognition of the name. "Ah, we know him well, but he is not here. Generally he stays aboard his yacht."

"Does he have a dinner reservation?" she asked.

"No, *signorina*, not at this time."

She breathed a little sigh of relief and retired to her room, where she checked in with Anna back at the operations center in California to get an update on any new intelligence on her mission. She advised Anna that she believed that she would be entering a highly secure environment the next day, and therefore it would be some time before they could communicate again.

Anna also had some interesting information for Nadia. "Nadia, there is something else that might interest you. There has been a development in the Bartolini matter. Following your successful mission, Bartolini, along with his in-house legal counsel and his CFO, did not want to disclose to the Board of Directors that they had been defrauded out of $30 million and lost out on the strategic investment deal. So they covered up the loss and sent another $30 million to Xanda Media, Inc.

"The joint venture with his company has realized remarkable early success over the last year, and Xanda just went public yesterday at a valuation exceeding a billion dollars. Since Bartolini's firm owned 50 percent of Xanda, it has been a big winner for them. The company's stock is trading strongly in the aftermarket and Bartolini's company shares are worth over $500 million. In the end, he may forgive you for your transgressions."

Nadia let out a laugh that cleansed her of all the pent-up stress of recent days. *So that lucky guy not only came out of this unscathed, but he is actually prospering,* she mused to herself. *With any luck we'll meet again, and I'll have some fun with that arrogant Italian.*

# CHAPTER 10

# INSURGENCY IN CYBERSPACE

THE NEXT MORNING A CAR AND driver appeared at the hotel and took Nadia to Russoff's villa. The car wound its way up the hill overlooking Porto Cervo to an area near the top. The villa was located at the end of a long driveway in a walled compound. At the entrance to the compound, at a gate, they were stopped by two heavily-armed guards in military-looking uniforms.

"Who is the woman?" one of the guards asked the driver.

"Weren't you notified?" the driver responded testily. "She is an addition to Russoff's team at the compound."

The guard eyed Nadia suspiciously and jerked his head toward the guard shack next to the gate. The other guard went inside and thumbed through some papers. He returned, saying that there was a record of her expected arrival, but they had to do a security check.

Nadia had a handbag and a small suitcase. The guards searched through both bags meticulously and found nothing.

"Where is your cell phone?" one demanded.

"I don't have one," she replied.

"Nonsense! Everyone has one," he insisted.

"If you must know, the police took it from me on the mainland," she replied. "They wanted it for evidence or some investigation they were doing on me. That was before your people snatched me out of there."

The guard walked back to the guard shack, and Nadia overheard the two guards arguing in Russian, in a hushed tone, about something.

It was becoming a heated debate, and she could barely make out what they were saying. But it appeared that they were arguing over which one of them would get to perform a strip search on her. A coin was tossed, and the stockier of the two guards laughed lasciviously.

"Please step out of the vehicle and go into the guard shack, miss," he said.

She complied. There, the guard performed a body search that gave new meaning to the word "thorough."

"Is this necessary?" she protested. "It must be obvious that I have nowhere to hide anything."

"You would be wise not to give me any lip," the guard grunted. "Everything is okay. You are free to go."

Approaching the villa, Nadia could see that it was also well guarded by security forces. She had no doubt that they would not hesitate to do her harm, if they found out her true identity.

It was frightening to her. She was entering the domain of a powerful, ruthless oligarch. She twisted the little garnet ring on her finger, a habit that she had developed when she was nervous or sensed danger. Nadia hoped that the gypsy, decades earlier, had truly empowered the ring as she had claimed. She would need its protection.

Her car drove down a long driveway to a motor court in front of the villa. As she stepped out of the car, she was greeted by Mikhail Andropov, who introduced himself as Russoff's Project Manager. He wasted no time getting into the business of the project.

"Our project carries the code name *VedaX*. Its name is derived from the ancient Sanskrit word '*veda*,' meaning 'knowledge,' and paired with '*X*,' the multiplication sign," he explained. "They think of it as *knowledge multiplied*."

The villa was a sprawling, single-story Mediterranean structure constructed mostly out of stone, perhaps from the local terrain, which had an abundant supply of it. It had a swimming pool, manicured landscaping, and a commanding view of Maddalena Bay.

*View of Maddalena Bay from Villa*

Mikhail escorted her past the villa to a separate building inside the compound. There were a number of high-tech antennas on top of the structure. The building had only light-story windows located high on the walls to allow light in, but not to allow anyone to see in or out. Guards were posted at its entrance. It was there that Project *VedaX* was housed. As Nadia might have expected, the project space was equipped with sophisticated computer and communications facilities. It had a satellite link to bypass the unreliable terrestrial network that was heavily monitored by the Italian government.

Nadia would be the fourth member of the very small team working on Russoff's special project. With Mikhail, there were two others, known only by their first names: Nicholas and Rajat, who was simply called "Raj." They were both very young, brilliant coders but had little understanding of the systems aspects of the project. Nicholas, of course, was Russian, but Raj was from India. He had graduated from the prestigious IIT, Indian Institute of Technology. Mikhail was in his mid-thirties and had a commanding understanding of the systems and communications issues. He was a little less conversant in the critical particulars of how the financial systems worked at big banks and at the US Federal Reserve System. That's where Nadia came in.

"Our team has been together for over a year," Mikhail explained. "We are working on a mission to break into the Federal Reserve's

Open Market operations and redirect approximately one billion American dollars into Russoff's secret offshore account in the Cayman Islands."

In effect, they sought to raid the US Treasury auction that took place periodically. However, because of the sophisticated firewalls that provided security for the Federal Reserve's systems and the team's lack of expertise in how those financial systems worked, they were finding this to be a very difficult challenge. They hoped that Nadia could help.

With Raj and Nicholas observing, Mikhail brought Nadia up to speed on the progress that they had made and the obstacles that they had run up against. The Russian FSB Agency had provided them with a software platform for cyber insurgency that they were adapting for Russoff's mission.

Nadia thought, *if the VedaX project successfully develops this technology, the FSB could take it back from Russoff, and it could be a powerful weapon to disrupt the US financial system. No wonder the CIA is highly concerned.*

She questioned her new colleagues. "Why have you chosen such a difficult target? The Treasury Automated Auction Processing System, or TAAPS, is a very well-fortified electronic processing system for the sale of US Treasuries. There are other, easier targets, such as the large commercial banks."

"Mr. Russoff has pointed to the fact that the US Treasury runs 200 auctions and sells over $4 trillion of securities each year," Mikhail explained. "He says the United States would never miss a billion dollars—they would just print more.

"The purchase and sale of US Treasuries used to be conducted entirely through a very laborious paper system. Years ago it had been converted to an all-electronic system. Russoff believes that there is a way to break in, reroute the funds into his account, and cover our tracks."

"It would be easier to launch a coordinated simultaneous attack on multiple banks, taking smaller amounts from each, and still get our targeted billion-dollar payday," Nadia suggested.

Mikhail nodded. "Perhaps. But we have our orders and need to find out how to pull it off."

"Specifically, what have you done so far?" she asked.

"We have hacked into the Federal Reserve website and placed intelligence gathering Internet worms in the TAAPS system," he explained. "These can be activated at our command. However, the accounts of big purchasers of Treasuries are protected by a sophisticated Security Socket Layer, or SSL as it is called, with complex algorithmic cryptographic security codes. These codes are changed dynamically, and we have not been able to break them."

"We will need to download the activity from the Internet worms and input the data into our computers here," Nadia suggested. "Perhaps then, using pattern recognition analytical techniques, we can break the codes."

Nadia, Mikhail, and their two colleagues continued to work on the challenging problem of their electronic funds transfer insurgency. They worked virtually around the clock. However, as a diversion from the intense mental exertion the project demanded, Nadia would swim laps in the villa's pool every morning. She had learned to swim when she was in college, and it was the one physical activity that she enjoyed most.

During what little free time they had, Nicholas and Raj enjoyed playing Kriegspiel, a variation on the game of chess, but more daring and faster-moving. In the game of Kriegspiel, a player can only see their own pieces. A barrier is placed between the competitors, blocking their view of the other's board. A third person acts as the referee, instructing the players when it is their turn to move and whether the move is "legal" or "illegal." Players execute moves in an effort to deduce where their opponent's pieces are placed.

The days went by quickly, and before Nadia knew it, a few weeks had passed. It was now mid-summer, and the Costa Smeralda was booming with activity. The little insurgency team, however, was confined to Russoff's villa, under tight control. Despite their seclusion, it was a good place to work, with the Mediterrean climate, exquisite views, and delectable cuisine being outstanding perks of the job.

During this time, the team grew closer together. Nadia learned that Mikhail's father, mother, and sister worked for Russoff's company at a plant in Russia. Russoff intentionally employed family members of key people in "sensitive, high security jobs" to assure him of their undivided loyalty. If they turned on him in any way, their family would suffer severe consequences. Through this practice, he had a very tight grip on his most important employees.

Working long hours in an intimate setting, Nadia reveled in the camaraderie of this small coterie. The activities of the day were not complicated by a gender-based agenda. Nicholas and Raj were very bright computer programmers and derived a lot of satisfaction in solving complex logic and mathematical problems. She shared that interest with them, and it was enjoyable to engage with others of high intellectual capacity. But there was always the oversight of Russoff's security operations and the risk of discovery.

Ivan Slutsky was the Managing Director of Russoff's Security Operations. He was a physically imposing man, with a strong build and a square jaw. He had a jagged scar on his cheek and tattoos of serpents on his arms. A glance from Slutsky's beady black , unblinking eyes, as cold as a snake's, would chill one's soul. All of Russoff's staff, even his bodyguards, feared Slutsky. He had served in the KGB before it was dissolved and knew Russoff's father. Perhaps it was his job, but Slutsky seemed suspicious of everything and trusted no one.

He had been in charge of the due diligence investigations on Nadia. Although the effort had turned up nothing that did not check out, nothing that compromised her, he was uncomfortable with the lack of available information about her past. There were good records in France, but he could not trace much about her in Russia. Because she had been an orphan, there was no name or family name for her; no official records were available. It all seemed logical, but still the absence of information bothered him.

*What about that cell phone that had reportedly been confiscated by the police in France?* he thought. *If I could get my hands on it, I might be able to shed some light on her story.*

It also bothered him that he could not find any newspaper articles about her husband's disappearance. Surely an international incident of this kind would have engendered wide coverage in the media.

Russoff was conflicted over Nadia. She was not a trusted employee that had been thoroughly vetted, yet he needed her. She was essential to the mission. He asked Slutsky to stay close to Nadia, to monitor her daily activities and continue to dig for more information. Slutsky relocated from Russoff's headquarters in Moscow to the villa in Porto Cervo while the cyber-attack project was ongoing.

Periodically he would approach Nadia and ask her questions about her past. This made her nervous … very nervous.

One day Slutsky approached her and asked, "Nadia, I am troubled by the fact that there were no newspaper reports of your husband's abduction in Paris. Can you explain that to me?"

"My husband worked for a defense contractor. I was never quite sure what he did," she said evenly, keeping her cool despite Slutsky's brusque manner. "After his disappearance I was contacted by the US military attaché in Paris and instructed not to report any details to the press. They told me that it was a matter of national security, and they were endeavoring to get him back. They said if I leaked it to the press, it would jeopardize their efforts to recover him. So I complied with their instructions."

Slutsky stared menacingly at her. Even his face had muscles that clenched and unclenched like a restless nest of vipers. "I see. What did you do when he did not return?"

"I was in a difficult situation," she said. "I could not go to the French police. I suspected that there was more to it than I knew. At some point I was told that an insurgent group had captured him and was demanding ransom. I was suspicious that I was not getting the whole story or, perhaps, even the truth, but there was nothing I could do."

"How did that all end?"

"Eventually, I was contacted by a member of the State Department who told me that the effort to secure my husband's release had failed. They said that the United States does not pay ransom money, and that the insurgents had killed him.

"I was devastated and angry," she explained. "I was alone and needed to go on with life without him. Fortunately, I had a job and could support myself."

This seemed to satisfy Slutsky, at least for the moment. However, he would continue to persist in asking questions whenever he could. Nadia was concerned that any mistake could put her life at risk.

The team continued to work relentlessly on the project, but the challenges were great, and they would often run into problems that seemed unsolvable. The US Treasury and banking system were well fortified with many layers of security barriers. At times they would become frustrated. They wondered if their task was doable?

One day, sensing that they had come to an impasse, Nadia thought that it would be good for the team to take a break from their intensive coding work.

"Let's take the afternoon off and get some exercise." She proposed that they take a hike through the hills higher up on the island, above the villa, looking out over the Mediterranean.

"That's a great idea!" Mikhail enthused. Nicholas and Raj heartily concurred.

Russoff's security guards would not allow them to go into town without being heavily "supervised." There was a trailhead close to the villa and a path that led to and across a ridge higher up on the steep hillside. They all dressed in shorts, T-shirts, and running shoes.

Nadia wore black silk shorts and a dark red tank top cut off at the midriff. This was quite different than the slacks and T-shirt that they saw her in every day.

They hiked up the trail to the top of the northernmost hill on the island. It presented a fabulous view of the surrounding sea and the small islands that dotted the Costa Smeralda coastline. From their vantage point they could see Corsica off in the distance, perhaps even the legendary port of Bonafacio.

This thirty-mile stretch of seafront property, arguably one of the most beautiful areas on the planet, had been acquired in 1961 by His Highness Prince Aga Khan IV. Over the years that followed he developed it with a keen sense for the environment. All structures have low profiles and blend seamlessly into their natural surroundings.

Nadia, Mikhail, Nicholas, and Raj sat down to rest and drink some water while enjoying the view. Nadia wanted to know more about them. They had had very little social time together because of their rigorous work schedule.

"Mikhail, do you live in Moscow?" she asked.

"Yes, I have a home near Russoff's corporate headquarters."

"Are you married?"

Mikhail smiled broadly at the question. "Da, I have a wife and a young boy. My regular job is in the IT Department of Mr. Russoff's headquarters operation. This is the first time I have had an assignment away from home. I have been away for too long, and I miss my family."

Nadia thought that it was good to see a young man like Mikhail that had a happy marriage and continued to have a strong love for his wife. In spite of being away from his home now for a protracted period, he had not seized on the opportunity, when working closely with her, to seek out a relationship. That showed an element of character that she admired in him. He was not like the Russian men that she had known.

"How has it been for you, working for Russoff?" she asked.

Mikhail's face turned to stone. "We do not talk about it. He is a difficult man and a tough taskmaster. But I have a very good, well-paying job, and I am grateful for it."

He paused for a moment, and seeing Nadia's expectant look, decided it was safe to expound on his situation to his friend.

"I have always been a loyal employee and never had any problems with Russoff. He trusts me. However, I have heard many stories about how he came to own his two large companies. His father was a high-ranking general in the KGB and a member of the Politburo. He had enormous power. During the privatization period that followed the collapse of the Soviet Union, a number of large companies were being passed into private hands, and there was a power struggle among Soviet leaders on who would get those huge assets.

"Vladimir's father, General Russoff, had the foresight to see what might be coming and had sent his son off to get a good education. He graduated from a business school in England years before the collapse and privatization movement. So he was well positioned to run the companies.

"However, with many Soviet leaders looking to get control of a few choice companies, those assets went to the strong and ruthless individuals in the country's power structure. Others that sought to acquire those companies were often killed, had family members abducted until they succumbed … and others just disappeared, probably to Siberia. Those that survived and ended up with the large state enterprises had to be very tough guys and brutal in dealing with their competition.

"In Russia, there is no 'demarcation line' between political power and the ownership of private sector assets. It is incredibly corrupt and has created an enormous concentration of wealth and power among the *elithy*—the wealthy elite. It seems likely that Russoff's father was behind the events that led to his ownership of the companies, but there is no way to know what role he might have played himself."

Mikhail paused a moment to let Nadia digest this information and then went on.

"Also, there was Ivan Slutsky. He worked in General Russoff's military command for years before becoming the head of security operations for Vladimir. He probably was the 'trigger man' on the actions that eliminated much of Russoff's competition. So, Nadia, you do not want to get on his bad side."

*He is already suspicious of me*, she thought with considerable anxiety. *I have good reason to worry and to avoid him as much as possible.*

"There is another thing that we need to be concerned about," Mikhail whispered. "Nicholas and Raj are on loan from the cyber warfare unit of the FSB. I suspect that the organization may have an interest in what Russoff is up to, and they are shadowing our activities. They might seek to take over the project and abduct our whole team. Who knows where they would take us. On the other hand, it is not likely that they would cross Mr. Russoff."

Nicholas overheard Mikhail's comment and rebutted. "When I was re-assigned from the FSB, I was not told to do anything for them."

"Still, they might be watching us ... tracking what we are doing," Mikhail said.

"Raj, what about you?" Nadia asked. "How did you end up on the team?"

"I graduated from the Indian Institute of Technology with honors and had many opportunities in India. I was offered a job in the cyber intelligence operations of the FSB, the Federal Security Service of the Russian Federation. More specifically, I was assigned to the Federal Agency for Government Communications and Information, the FAPSI agency, which is responsible for foreign electronic surveillance. I preferred to stay in India, but the Russian offer was too lucrative. I send most of my pay back to my family in India. They are very poor, and the money keeps them and many in our village from starving.

"I am fascinated by the intricacies of the Internet," he continued. "The job offered to me was much more interesting than the typical programming assignments that I might have received at Infosys or one of the other Indian companies. However, I am a little uncomfortable with the clandestine aspects of the assignments that I have with the bureau. I desperately need this job, but at times I am challenged ethically by what we do in Russia."

Nadia turned to Nicholas. "It's your turn, Nick—how did you end up on this project?"

"Like Raj, I was recruited to join the FSB. My family lives in Krasnoda, near the Black Sea. My father is an industrial worker, but I had the opportunity to attend Moscow University and graduated at the top in my class. The FSB was the best opportunity offered to me when I graduated. Mr. Russoff is deeply connected with the political powers in Moscow and arranged for Raj and me to be redirected on a temporary assignment to this project."

Nadia could empathize with these affable, idealistic young men, and she liked them all tremendously. Like her, Raj and Nicholas had experienced poverty in their youth. The four of them soaked up rays and chatted away most of the afternoon. It was a pleasant interlude from the difficult work schedule that they were on.

In a quiet moment Nadia thought about what she was doing and what outcome she might orchestrate. How could she rationalize Russoff getting such a large amount of money out of this enterprise? She had put into place the means to destroy the entire software and Internet system that could extract funds from the US Treasury auction. All she needed to do was to effectively "pull the trigger" on the programming mechanism that she had secretly embedded in the system. However, her thoughts turned to the consequences.

If she caused the mission to fail, Russoff would be furious and would surely order the execution of the entire team. While she believed that she could escape, there was no way out for Mikhail, Nicholas, and Raj. She did not want severe harm to come to them. *Perhaps there is a way to solve this dilemma,* she mused. *I could go ahead with the cyber-attack, completing the mission, but could then destroy the system once it was successful. That might be a way to save my colleagues from Russoff's retribution.*

*Porto Cervo harbor at dusk*

Looking down on the coastline they could see many large yachts anchored in the harbor. *Who were these people?* They thought. Owing to their impoverished backgrounds, it was difficult to fathom the enormous wealth that some men had. They were curious how those people had acquired so much.

"It is getting late, and we'd better get back to the villa," Mikhail said.

So this motley crew headed back to the villa, stopping on occasion to look out over the harbor scene as the sun went down.

Work continued in earnest the next day. They were homing in on a solution, a clever way to pull off the cyber heist. Nadia got up from her workstation to stretch and get a breath of air; she was confronted by Slutsky at the door. He had continued to try to get information about her past and, in particular, her husband. Her answers were too vague. It was not adding up for him. It kept gnawing on him that there had to be more to the story. There was something he didn't know.

He pulled Nadia outside and shut the door behind them. "I need more information; you have been too evasive," he demanded. "Tell me about your husband."

"I have grown weary of your interrogations, Slutsky," she said bravely. "I am only trying to do my job, and you should be doing yours, not continually harassing me."

Slutsky stood stock-still, his eyes never blinking, as the corners of his straight slit of a mouth curled in a mockery of a smile. "You have a big mouth … and a pretty one. It would be a shame for it to get ruined. Answer my question!"

"My husband, Jack Pearson, worked for SAIC, a large American contract research firm that did a lot of top-secret work for the government," she admitted. "He headed up the company's Paris office, and I was told that he had been working on covert terrorism missions when he was abducted."

"Go on."

"That's all I know. My husband would never tell me much. I did not want to get into the specifics because I thought that you might be suspicious of me. If you want, I am sure you can check with the company, SAIC."

"Perhaps. All I know is, comrade, you do not fit in here. You are too much of an unknown to be in such a vital position."

Without warning he shoved her against the wall with a force that nearly knocked the wind out of her delicate body.

"Who are you?" he spluttered. "Was your husband an American spy? Are *you* a spy? Answer me!"

Nadia struggled to get her breath. Slutsky's thumbs dug into her throat, and she could feel his sweaty fingers probing her face.

"If Russoff did not believe that you were critical to this project, I would get rid of you now!"

At last he released his grip, and Nadia fell away from him, gasping and coughing. "I am just a simple working girl, trying to get ahead," she said in a croaking voice. "I did not come here on my own. You abducted me."

"*Simple* you are not!" Slutsky fumed, pushing her hard against the wall again. "Tell me, simple one, how could a former bank employee know so much about covert cyber operations and cryptography and have such a high level of computer knowledge? This is the kind of expertise that only skilled operatives would have."

Mikhail and the others had heard the commotion and rushed to Nadia's aid. They had bonded with Nadia and cared about her. They were shocked by Slutsky's brutality and despised the fact that he had it in for her.

"Ivan, remember she is Russian, not American! We need her on this project," Nicholas pleaded.

"Nicholas, you stay out of this!" Slutsky said.

"You know my background at Banco Paribas," Nadia said. "You know of my schooling in computer science and mathematics."

"You were only there for a few years. That's child's play compared to what you are doing here," Slutsky said with increased skepticism.

"I am a fast learner," she said.

"Bah! No one is *that* fast a learner. I don't buy it!"

"For me it comes easily. I was fortunate to be born with a pretty good mind," she said. "How can I convince you? Would you like a demonstration?"

"What do you mean … demonstration?" Slutsky said suspiciously.

"Nicholas, do we have a telephone directory?" Nadia asked.

"Do you mean a printed one?"

Nadia couldn't resist getting in a sly dig at Slutsky's expense. "Yes, it's the only kind that Slutsky would know how to use."

The four colleagues, with Slutsky in tow, went inside the computer lab. Nicholas promptly dug a telephone directory out of the files and handed it to Nadia.

"Here, pick any two numbers out of the directory," she said, turning to Slutsky and shoving the phone book at him. "Read them to me and Nicholas at the same time. He can enter them in the computer. Then, he can hit the multiply key to get the product of the two numbers. I will do the calculation in my head and write down the answer."

"Those are six-digit numbers. It can't be done," Slutsky insisted.

"If I can do it, will you get off my back?" she said.

"Ack, very well! Show me your damn trick … your *demonstration*!"

Slutsky then read off the two telephone numbers. "The first number is 939 475. The second number is 486 062."

Nicholas put them into the computer and mistakenly hit the divide key, instead of the multiply key.

"Sorry, I hit the division key by accident!" he apologized.

"Did you enter the first number first, before the second and the divisor key?" Nadia asked.

"Correct."

"No matter. Then I will do the division calculation instead," said Nadia to their amazement.

She wrote down a very long number on the piece of paper and read it off to the group, "1.9328295—is that correct?"

Slutsky and Nicholas looked at the computer screen and could not believe what they saw. The numbers were identical!

"I'm still skeptical, but clearly you do have some exceptional skills," Slutsky admitted. "Perhaps Russoff has truly found the missing link for the project team. Perhaps we should take Nadia to Monte Carlo and hit the casinos," he added somewhat jokingly.

A little later, word came to them that Russoff was coming to Sardinia and wanted an update on the project. He would meet Nadia and Mikhail at the Cala di Volpe for dinner. That evening a car and driver picked them up and took them to the hotel.

Russoff had arranged for a table in a quiet corner location of the restaurant. He made small talk then asked, cynically, about how they were enjoying the summer in Sardinia. He then quickly turned to their project.

"How is Project *VedaX* coming?" he asked, signaling his impatience.

Mikhail spoke up. "Nadia has been a valuable addition to our team. We have been working hard, but this is a difficult challenge."

"We are making good progress," Nadia offered and endeavored to provide more detail. "We have successfully inserted spyware in the Automated Clearing House, or ACH, that processes electronic funds transfer transactions in America. A big part of our work is to break the password codes that facilitate bids in the Treasury auction process and the purchase transactions. These passwords are complex cryptographic codes and change dynamically."

She was about to continue when Russoff held up his hand. "Enough! Spare me the boring technical aspects of the project. The bottom line is do you think that you can succeed in this mission?"

Mikhail and Nadia looked at each other and told him, with time, they believed that it was possible.

"Time is infinite, but my patience is not," said Russoff threateningly. "Do not test it. Give me the results I demand, or see *your* time come to an end."

As their dinner conversation proceeded, Nadia noticed a familiar man seated with three other yachtsmen at another table across the room. It was unmistakably Roberto Bartolini. This could be big trouble for her, if her identity were compromised. But she also knew that she was in the company of a man that Roberto probably respected … perhaps even feared. The mega-yacht community was a close-knit group, and they all knew each other, or at least about each other. *I am probably safe*, she thought.

At some point Roberto looked her way. He was stricken by her resemblance to Tatyana. But this woman had raven black hair and Tatyana was a blonde. *She might have bleached her hair when she was in San Francisco*, he thought. But he had no idea what had happened to her. Had she returned to Russia? What would she be doing here? Just the thought that he might cross paths with her again aroused him.

Roberto certainly recognized Russoff. He had the big black-hulled yacht in the harbor near the *Invictus*. Roberto knew Russoff by reputation. He was a bad guy and could be ruthless in dealing with opponents. The Russian was not one to fool around with. Roberto could tell that Russoff was engaged in a serious conversation and noted what looked like several members of Russoff's security staff in the background area of the restaurant. He dared not approach their table and confront the lady, but he was filled with curiosity. Could it be her? His heart—and libido—began to throb.

Eventually, Russoff, Mikhail, and Nadia finished their dinner and rose to leave. They had to pass near Roberto's table in their path out of the restaurant. As they approached Roberto's table, Nadia daringly looked straight at him. Their eyes met. Nadia's piercing, deep blue eyes penetrated his very being. It was as if a bolt of electricity had run through his body.

He remembered that look from a year earlier when he had played poker with her for "the rights to her body." He had never succeeded in that quest, but the obsession had lived within him ever since. He had never felt such sexual energy and always wondered what it would be like to experience her, a woman who was vastly his intellectual superior.

Now, as this near perfect replica of her walked by, he gazed at her. A subtle smile moved across her face as if to say, "You know who I am, but you can't touch me."

Chills ran down his spine as he realized that it might actually be her.

Back at Russoff's villa, they were beginning to home in on a way to pull off the cyber heist. The computer analysis of password activity had discovered a pattern that would allow them to attach a control code that would ride on top of a buyer's electronic bid and purchase transaction in a Treasury auction. With that code they could redirect the payment funds to an alternative destination. They could also send an electronic receipt to the buyer acknowledging the payment and crediting the buyer's account with the purchased Treasuries. Everything would look normal to both the Automated Auction Processing System and to the buyer. The US Treasury would have a record of the receipt of the incoming payment funds and the issuance of the Treasury bonds.

But the money would not be there.

With the low level of bureaucratic competence and sloppy accounting in the Bureau of Public Debt of the Treasury Department, perhaps they would never discover that the funds account did not balance. If the accountants did discover the accounts imbalance, it would be a puzzle that they could not resolve. If the funds from the auction did not match the cash in the US Treasury, they would think that it must be lost somewhere in the system. All of the records would be in order, but some of the money would be gone.

Now they needed to target one of the upcoming auctions and obtain from Russoff the bank account information into which they would transfer the funds. Nadia was also thinking about her own Swiss bank account.

The Russoff project was only part of the challenge here. She also had a task to do for the CIA and Olga. These seemed incompatible. How could she neutralize the cyber insurgency threat and also satisfy Russoff so as not to get "eliminated"? Also, she did not want harm to come to Mikhail and the two young software engineers on the team, all of whom had become like brothers to her.

Nadia contacted Russoff on a secure private line that he had made available to her.

"I believe that we are ready to go," Nadia announced.

"Very good," said Russoff. "I am impressed and pray for your sake that it will work."

"I will need the detailed information on the account into which you wish to transfer the funds."

"I do not want any record, electronic or otherwise, of the transaction so I must give it to you in person," Russoff said. "I will send my plane to Olbia to fly you back to the airport at Nice, where my driver will pick you up and bring you to my place at Antibes. There we will enjoy a private dinner together, and I will provide you with wire transfer instructions and all the account information that you need to complete the transaction.

"But you must not share this with anyone else, not even the team. If you do, you put your life at risk. Do you understand?"

"Perfectly! I have understood that from the beginning. You can be certain that there will be no compromise with the security of your account information."

When she arrived at Russoff's villa in Antibes there was a nice room waiting for her overlooking the sea. Nadia changed into her sapphire blue silk dress that matched her eye color. She stood there looking at herself in a mirror, turning this way and that. She loved the way that silk flowed across the subtle, sensuous curves of her figure. The diaphanous material was soft against her skin but also showed every detail of her beautiful body. She liked to wear this dress without any undergarment that might distract one's eye from the pureness of her lines. She added the simple diamond heart necklace and was then ready to meet Russoff.

She walked downstairs to the main salon where she was greeted by the villa's butler, who escorted her to the main terrace. It was where she had first met Russoff. She was served a glass of champagne and told that he would join her shortly.

A dining table for two had been set up on the terrace. It was dusk and the evening light was growing dim. The table was lit with candles, and it looked like a perfect scene for a man to seduce a young woman. Perhaps ninety feet below the rocky cliff, on which the terrace was perched, was the *Russian Five*. The lights on the big yacht were all turned on and reflected across the water. It was a mesmerizing scene.

From the villa's sound system, she could hear the music of an all-male Cossack chorus singing a cappella. The rich texture of the tenors and baritone voices was augmented by the sonorous rumble of the low-register bass members of the chorus. This was deeply masculine music and classic Russian. Nadia thought, *This music is filled with testosterone! What is a fragile feline creature like me doing in the lion's den?* Her heart started racing faster with a surge of fear and anticipation.

Russoff arrived and greeted her cordially. They were seated and he stated the obvious, that they needed a very private location to meet and discuss the details of the mission … and specifically for him to provide her with the vital account information to his offshore bank.

Russoff was more than twenty years her senior. While he was not an unattractive man, neither was he handsome in a traditional sense. He was a large, rugged man. Physically, Nadia was not attracted to him, yet she found him to be a fascinating man. His worldly experiences, breadth of knowledge, and attitudes were engaging. However, she feared him and knew that, at his will, he could have her erased. This was not a man to fool around with.

A waiter arrived and poured a familiar wine into the glasses on the table. It was her favorite: Corton-Charlemagne. How could he know? Only Olga knew of her preference. *It must be a coincidence*, she thought, *or somehow my identity has been compromised.*

"Mr. Russoff, I am curious. Why do you want to do this?" she asked nervously. "You obviously have a great deal of money. Another billion dollars will not make a difference, but carrying out this mission has its dangers, if you are caught."

Russoff shrugged his heavy shoulders. "I am intrigued with daring enterprises," he said, waving his hand insouciantly. "Some people may find challenge in climbing mountains. Some express their daring in sky-diving. My adventure is in doing things in the financial world that no one would believe could be accomplished. I do it for the sport of it. I love *the game*."

"I like that! I, too, am an adventurer of an unconventional sort." Nadia raised her wine glass in a toast and said, "Then we shall do this for the sport of it!"

Russoff smiled.

"Mr. Russoff, how did you acquire this fabulous property?"

"I was looking for the best location on the Mediterranean and asked my helicopter pilot to take me on a tour of the coastline," he explained. "When we passed over this place, I knew it was perfect. My agent offered the family that owned it a very generous price. But they said that it was not for sale—at any price. It had been in their family for seven generations, and they planned to keep it in the family.

"Their only daughter was abducted, and later I approached them to offer my assistance. I told them that we, in Russia, have ways of accomplishing things that are far more effective than the French police. But, I told them, if I get your daughter back, you must sell me the villa. Eventually, they reluctantly agreed since the police offered very little prospect of finding their daughter. Of course I was able to secure her safe return."

"Did you have anything to do with the abduction?" Nadia said, suspecting that he had been behind it all.

"You are a suspicious young lady." Russoff cracked a slight smile and then changed the subject. "Let's talk about our business project."

He told her that the next Treasury auction date was the following week and asked if the project team would be ready.

"Yes, we are in an all-systems-go mode," she reported. "What do you plan to do for the team, if we are successful?"

"Mikhail will be relocated to my headquarters' IT Department with a bonus and a big raise in his salary. Nicholas and Raj will also receive a generous bonus from me, but must return to their government posts, since they were only on loan to me from the government security division. I will take care of them. For you, Nadia, I will pay a bonus of $500,000, and you can have a permanent position in the Finance Department of my headquarters."

"That would be a lot of money for me—a big incentive to get it right. I am confident that we will succeed."

Their conversation continued through dinner on a range of subjects. At some point, she asked about his personal life.

"Are you married?"

"Yes, I am. I have a wife and three children. My wife lives in our home near Moscow, but I am rarely there. My business and other interests take me all over the world. While I have many homes, my favorite is right here in Antibes."

"Do you not miss your wife and children?"

"Our children are adults now, off living their own lives, and I have a somewhat Russian-style marriage with my wife. I provide a very good living for her, but we live separately and have done so for years."

Their lively conversation continued throughout a wonderful dinner prepared by Russoff's chef: a cold gazpacho soup to begin and Dover sole as the main course. The Corton Charlemagne was perfect with the Dover sole, but Nadia was carried away and drank too much of it. Nadia had consumed more wine than she was accustomed to and was feeling its effects. Romantic music began to flow across the terrace. As Russoff looked across the table at Nadia in the glow of the candle light, he thought, *My God, what a gorgeous woman!*

"Would you like to dance?" Russoff asked.

How could she refuse?

Up to this point, Russoff had shown little interest in her, other than for the cyber-attack project. He had always been cool and business-like toward her. After this much time in the presence of a man, she could always feel their attraction to her. She would know that she was capable of seducing them at will. None of that was visible with Russoff. He remained aloof. It made no difference to her since her plan was to keep her distance from him and to not complicate the mission with any sexual or romantic issues.

As they came together to dance, she felt his firm embrace. He had a great sense of the music and was a very good dancer. He pulled her close to him. This was a different sensation for her. She was used to being in control and used to engaging with men of weaker fortitude. She was accustomed to being the provocateur, the pursuer. The firmness with which he held her was surprisingly sensual.

This was an interesting encounter between a strong, powerful, dominant male and an enticing, brilliant beauty. Unexpectedly, she was becoming sexually aroused by this experience. This was not a romantic engagement with a man—it was a carnal passion that was exciting her. Nadia was becoming acutely aware that Russoff was very skilled at this ... and she was sinking into submission.

Her role was always as the predator, the seducer. Now the roles were reversed. Even though she was not attracted to him, some other powerful primal drive was taking over. It was not in her plan, but that night she would submit to his will. In a strange, intriguing sort of way, the desire to have him had overcome her.

"I am starting to feel the effects of that wonderful wine that you served this evening," Nadia said, aware that her words were coming out slightly slurred. "My apologies for being a little unbalanced as we dance. Perhaps it's time for me to turn in for the night."

Indeed, Nadia had consumed too much wine and was beginning to fade in spite of her growing desire to experience Russoff.

"As you wish," he said considerately. "Let me help you to your room!"

With that, he picked her up and carried her to her bedroom. It seemed effortless for him. She could feel Russoff's strength. The raw physicality of his strength further aroused her, but she was close to passing out.

Upon reaching her room he gently laid her down on the bed. Her head was spinning from the effects of too much alcohol for her fragile 118-pound body to absorb. He reached behind her neck, unhooked the clasp of her treasured diamond heart necklace. He placed it carefully on the side table next to the bed. Rolling her on to her side, he unzipped her dress, then slipped it off of her. When she had first arrived on the terrace, he had admired the way her simple silk dress clung closely to the contours of her body, uninterrupted, perhaps, by the signs of undergarments. So it was no surprise when his suspicions were confirmed that she wore no bra or panties.

The sensation of being undressed by him was an arousing experience.

Then, unexpectedly, he folded the cover over her body out of respect for her modesty. At this point she had almost passed out and was all but helpless. He left the bedside and a few moments later, she heard the sound of the shower in her bathroom.

*Is he taking a shower to make himself more pleasing to me?* she thought. It seemed a contradiction for this tough guy to be considerate of her in that way. The very thought and suspense of the process that was unfolding caused an adrenalin rush that brought her back from the edge of unconsciousness.

Now Russoff stood at the end of the bed, naked save for the towel draped around his middle. He was a rugged, masculine-looking man. He had broad shoulders and a muscular chest and arms. Earlier Nadia had not been attracted to him, perhaps influenced by her fear of him. Now, in her groggy state, Nadia saw him in a different light. She gazed lustily at the beads of water still clinging to his magnificent physique.

From under the covers he picked up her feet and massaged them in a way that heightened the tactile pleasure of it. Nadia was surprised by the sensuality of his touch. He rested her feet on the towel around his midriff and massaged the calf muscles of her legs. From the contours of the towel she could see that he was getting excited. Her feet could feel that his arousal was in full form.

As her desire rose, so did her anxiety. She thought, *This is a very dangerous man. What am I doing?* Her simultaneous feeling of fear and carnal arousal made for a strange, conflicting mix of emotions.

Dropping the towel on a chair, he peeled away the cover and lay down beside her. The coolness of his skin and fresh smell from the shower was a pleasant sensation for her. He began to touch her, to caress her, but gently. He was in no hurry. Nadia could sense that he was an aesthete. He was carefully examining every detailed aspect of her figure. He was appreciating the extraordinary beauty of her flawless body in the way that a connoisseur might savor a great wine. For such a rugged and powerful man, this was quite unexpected.

His touch was not rough, nor was it passionate … it was strangely sensual in a different way. He was moving in a very controlled manner, not impatient like most men that she had known. The skillful, considerate way in which he touched her caused her anxieties to melt away. He looked into her deep blue eyes. He had turned his attention from the physical part of her and was penetrating into her inner self. It was as if her eyes were a window through which he could peer deep into her as a person. She felt vulnerable and, at the same time, excited.

He was after *the woman inside*.

It was true that Russoff had been intrigued with Nadia since their dinner at the Eden Roc restaurant in Antibes, when she had boldly confronted his CFO and articulately refuted his argument. He found her to be a very intelligent woman with a mysterious past and a willingness to walk on the dark side of the law. All this was fascinating to him and elevated the pleasure of the timeless encounter between a man and a woman that was unfolding with her.

He turned her onto her stomach and began running his hands across her back, pausing to explore the dimples above her derriere.

He continued down across her torso following every curve, as if to enjoy the full sensuality of the journey. She was highly sensitized and even the coolness of the sheets against her breasts, stomach, and thighs stimulated an erotic effect. When he touched the inside of her thighs, it was electrifying. She felt the tip of his member brushing against the side of her buttocks and bit her lip with desire. She was ready.

Russoff turned and threw one leg across her so as to straddle her from behind. He did not place the weight of his large body on her, but she could feel his presence over her. He kissed her back, then brushed her hair aside and kissed her neck and ear. Nadia now wanted to get on with it and arched her back, thrusting her derriere upward into him. No more invitation was necessary. Because he was almost twice her size, she feared that his entry might be painful. But the long period of foreplay had left them both highly lubricated, and he slipped inside of her easily.

Nothing Alexandra had taught her about sexual relationships with men had prepared her for this. Russoff did not fit any of the stereotypes that she had been prepared to encounter. As the pace of their intercourse escalated, his strength and masculinity accelerated her pleasure of the moment. In spite of the full pulsating engagement of their bodies, he was careful not to let his heavy weight rest on her, which could detract from her experience. His movements were slow and deliberate, as if to enjoy every tactile sensation of the moment. This was a very skillful lover.

He paused for a moment, and then turned her over. His eyes roved over every inch of her body, from the perfectly shaped breasts, across her flat tummy, and finally to the enticing triangle of maidenhair. He wanted to savor the beauty of this creature and to encounter her completely as a woman. Nadia let out a small gasp as he gently kissed her nipples. He remarked admiringly, "Marvelous!"

Russoff rolled over and stepped off the bed. He dragged her body toward the edge where he was standing. He lifted her and placed her head on a pillow to improve her comfort. Nadia knew where all this was headed and lifted her legs high, placing her calves on his shoulders. He slowly entered her and again looked into her deep blue eyes. Nadia felt the surge of his total passionate involvement with her. This, combined with the physicality of his unobstructed access to her body, amplified her own sexual arousal ... elevating it to new heights.

*The moment* was growing close and, for the first time, it seemed that Russoff was losing control and passion was taking over. She whispered something to him in Russian. Her voice was low, almost inaudible.

*What did she say?* He wondered. *It sounded like* "The game *is on!*" *If that was it, what did she mean?*

Whatever she said did not register with him. By this time his brain was not functioning normally; what was going on was purely biological. He could not think. The orgasmic process was accelerating.

Her body began to quiver as the pulse of things moved forward, with a clear path to conclusion. Her skin glowed pink in sweet anguish, a sex flush, with her blood raging through the veins and engulfing her body. Their climax came simultaneously, something she had never experienced before.

He collapsed on the bed beside her. For a while they lay there side by side while their heartbeats slowly wound down, back to normal. He pulled the cover back over her and slipped out of the room as she fell asleep.

The next morning there was a soft knock at the door to her room. One of Russoff's servants had brought a continental breakfast to her and some fresh flowers for her room. On the platter were a memory stick and a note.

The note said, *This is all the information that you need for the mission. Guard it with your life and destroy it after its use.*

There was no comment about the night before, but the server notified her that a car would be there in an hour to take her back to the airport and then on to Sardinia. Russoff had already left to return to his headquarters in Moscow. If she needed to, she could reach him there.

Nadia pondered her situation. Russoff had not developed an emotional attachment to her, nor she to him. The sex had been exciting for both of them, but that was where their personal relationship began and ended. She speculated that after the project was over he might decide to "delete" her, since she was not under his control as were the others on the team. She could not trust him. It was a very dangerous situation, and she would need a way out once the mission was complete. Knowing Russoff's powers, all the airports would be covered by his security staff. She would need a way off the island.

Back in Sardinia, Nadia and the team were embarking on a big push to implement all aspects of the process in order to pull off the "sting operation" on the upcoming US Treasury auction.

The team would need to monitor the incoming bids for the auction, and target only those that would succeed, since typically only about a third of bids were at a price level to be selected. On the day of the auction, things would happen very fast. Consequently, their team needed to set up a surveillance Internet worm configuration to observe the bidding in real time and select target bidders on which their insurgent code would ride. No one bid would be large enough for them to extract a billion dollars in a single transaction, so they would be selecting multiple targets at smaller amounts.

In the days leading up to the auction Nadia, Mikhail, and their small team were busy with preparations for their elegantly conceived heist. Nadia had personally developed some of the key modules. With the divided duties on the team, others knew of Nadia's programming components, but did not know what was in them or how they operated. Her special expertise in the inner workings of the electronic funds transfers systems and the Treasury auction process was critical to the function of their mission.

It was now their "D-Day," the day of the auction. The team was excited to see if they could pull it off. Nadia was confident. The system for their commercial insurgency was completely automated, so the team simply watched as events unfolded that day. Their computers were set up to monitor the progress of the auction and the flow of funds.

With the project nearing completion, Nadia had to consider the risk that Russoff might want to have her eliminated to cover any tracks of the heist. That risk was further elevated by actions that she planned to take once the project concluded. It was still her agenda to destroy the cyber threat once the mission was complete.

Mikhail, Nicholas, and Raj were employed by him and would be relocated back to Moscow, under his complete control. They did not pose a risk to him. She, however, did not plan to go to Moscow and therefore posed a potential security breach. Russoff could not simply let her leave and go on with her life. She needed a way out.

There was another thing that worried her even more. About a week earlier, two more men had arrived at the villa compound and were staying in Russoff's guesthouse. They often talked with Ivan Slutsky and seemed to be shadowing Nadia and the team. She was told that they were additional security, but Nadia suspected that there might be more to it.

Her fear was that the cyber warfare division of Russia's military was interested in their project. Nicholas and Raj were on loan from that organization, so it made sense that they knew about Russoff's ambitions. Her know-how and the system that the team had created would be a powerful tool in the hands of the wrong people.

As Nadia thought about this possibility, she concluded that it was highly likely that they intended to abduct her and take her, with the team, to a secret Russian military location where the cyber warfare operations were headquartered. They needed her and the software system to be able to launch attacks of their own on the US financial system. When they learned about her destruction of the system, the prospect of her capture would be certain.

In the basement where the tech operations were conducted, the team was elated as they saw the numbers marching across the screen, evidencing the flow of funds into Russoff's account. The assignment had been a big success. What they did not know was that Nadia had planted software functionality in the Internet worms to divert some funds into her own offshore account and planted a termination code in all of them to wipe out the whole system once the operation was concluded.

Mikhail approached Slutsky. "Ivan, our mission here was successfully completed this afternoon, and we have sent off our notice to Mr. Russoff," he said. "I am sure he will be happy. My team has worked hard and been cooped up here for months. It would be nice to have a little celebration tonight."

Slutsky's flinty expression softened a little. "What do you have in mind?"

"I know a little restaurant/bar down on the harbor," Mikhail said. "It is in the Porto Vecchio, the old port. It would be great to take the whole team down there for drinks and a nice dinner."

"I am responsible for the security of the group," Slutsky reminded him. "I would have to go with you. Mr. Russoff has instructed me to escort you all back to Moscow when the project is complete. Since you have notified him of its success, I'm sure his plane will be here tomorrow to pick us all up. He specifically told me to be sure that Nadia was aboard."

Mikhail smiled. "Of course it's fine that you join us, but you owe Nadia an apology for treating her so roughly and being overly suspicious of her."

Slutsky was becoming persuaded. "Perhaps I could share a toast with her if they have some good Russian vodka."

"Nicholas and I would enjoy that as well," Mikhail said. "If you permit me a few outside calls, I am sure I can arrange to have it there."

"No problem. Just make sure that there is an ample supply. My preference would be for Stolichnaya Elit vodka and have them make sure it is cold, very cold."

Mikhail told Nicholas, Raj, and Nadia of the plan for the evening and made the calls to arrange for several bottles of Stolichnaya Elit to be on ice at the restaurant.

It was wonderful for the team to have some social time together after their long work schedule on the project. As nice as the Costa Smeralda was, they hadn't seen much of it, and they were looking forward to leaving the island and getting back home.

At the restaurant things were pretty relaxed. Even Slutsky, who by nature was a very uptight man, was loose that evening.

"Four of us are Russian, and Raj, we will adopt you this evening," Slutsky declared. "I propose a toast to our homeland … to the world's greatest composers and the Czars that have given our country its culture and tradition."

Slutsky hoisted his glass and exclaimed, "*Do dna!*" in Russian, meaning drink the whole vodka down, or bottoms up.

And so there were toasts and more toasts and a few things to eat. The little coterie was having a good time together, even with the presence of "Ivan *the terrible*" as they called Slutsky behind his back.

As the evening wore on, Nadia excused herself. "Comrades, I am going to the ladies' room. Please do not drink all the vodka while I'm gone!" She got up and wobbled toward the restrooms in the back of the bar area.

Slutsky kept a close eye on her and commented to Mikhail, "Do you think that sexy little Nadia hates men?"

"Perhaps only you!" Mikhail said, laughing. "She has been very serious in working with my team of young men. She has not shown the female side of her in all the time we have worked together."

"She seems very happy tonight," Slutsky observed, his lust beginning to show. "Perhaps with a little more vodka, she might like me enough to extend the party with me into the night."

Mikhail shrugged noncommittally. "I guess all things are possible. I am seeing a much lighter side of her since the mission was completed successfully."

After some time had passed Slutsky wondered why Nadia had not returned. He walked to the back and knocked on the door of the ladies' room.

"Nadia, are you there?"

No answer came back. After repeated knocks and inquiry, he opened the door and looked in. There was no one there, but he did notice a window just big enough for a woman to crawl through. He ran out of the restaurant entrance and around to the back side. She was nowhere to be seen. Slutsky walked out on the dock adjacent to the restaurant. It was dusk and he had good visibility of the shoreline and the boats on the docks. He didn't see her anywhere.

He walked down on the dock to look around. There on the ground was something … a flimsy piece of fabric. He picked it up and immediately recognized it.

It was Nadia's dress, but she had disappeared.

It was early evening in Moscow when Russoff received the e-mail message from Nadia that he had been waiting for.

> *Dear Mr. Russoff,*
>
> *I greatly appreciate the opportunity that you have offered me. By the time you receive this, $1 billion will have arrived in your Cayman Islands account. For traceability purposes, I suggest that you immediately transfer the funds to a new location and close out the Cayman account.*
>
> *I have completed the project for you, but I am not one to linger in any one place for long, so I have moved on.*
>
> *The electronic insurgency system that we developed could be discovered by the American government at some time in the future.*

*This would be big trouble for you. For that reason I have taken measures to completely destroy it in order to cover our tracks. Immediately after the funds had been extracted from the US Treasury, the Internet worms and spyware planted there were programmed to self-destruct, leaving no trace that they were ever present. I have also programmed the systems that we developed at your villa in Sardinia to "blow up" and leave no trace behind. So you should be in good shape, although not be in a position to replicate the project.*

*Regarding the $500,000 bonus, please distribute it to my co-workers on the project team. In the extraction of funds from the Treasury auction, I took the liberty to add a ten percent commission for myself.*

*Nadia*

A ten percent commission—that's $100 million! Russoff had to smile at her moxie. What an extraordinary, mysterious woman. His brief encounter with Nadia had been a hyper-adventure and had succeeded in making him a lot of money. He wanted more of her, but it was not to be.

It was still office hours in the Cayman Islands, so Russoff called the president of the bank where the account had been set up. Russoff was anxious to check up on Nadia's report, so he asked for an update on the account balance. The bank president gave him the good news.

"Mr. Russoff, there has been an unusual amount of activity on your account. Earlier today there was a flood of wire transfers coming into the account and you now have a balance of over $1 billion. What would you like me to do with the money?"

"My CFO, Yuri Petrovski, will be in touch with you in the morning."

Russoff then called Petrovski at home.

"Yuri, do you remember that precocious young Russian woman that I recruited to our cyber insurgency team?"

"How could I ever forget her!"

"Well, with her help, the team just pulled off an amazing sting on the US Treasury auction, and we now have $1 billion of new cash in an account in the Cayman Islands. I am concerned about the traceability of the money back to our project, so first thing tomorrow I want you to close down the Cayman account and transfer the funds into my personal account in Moscow."

"You are a clever man," Yuri said. "I am on top of it and will take care of the transfer as soon as our banks open tomorrow. Can you provide me with the contact information for the bank in the Caymans?"

"I will e-mail it to you now." Russoff hung up.

The next day Yuri called the Cayman Islands bank president to arrange for the transfer of funds. The banker informed him that something strange had happened during the night: the funds had been transferred out of the account. No bank employee had been involved, but the account balance was back down to almost zero.

He explained, "Sometimes a transferring bank will recall funds directly from an account, if the transfer was mistaken. It came in mysteriously, so perhaps that explains it?"

"I don't think so," Yuri stated. "There must be an electronic record of where the funds were transferred to."

"Yes, let me check our records," replied the bank president.

Yuri could hear the clicking of a keyboard in the background as the bank president entered data into their computer system.

"Yes, here it is. The funds were transferred to a bank in Luxemburg. There is no name on the account, only a designation: SU-OIS-157864439."

"Thank you," Yuri replied. "I believe I know something about that account."

Yuri hung up and called his boss. "Mr. Russoff, we have a problem. Someone tapped into the Cayman account and took our money."

"How is that possible? Do you think it was Nadia? She was the only other person to know about it," Russoff speculated.

Yet it troubled him. Nothing pointed to Nadia. After all, she had already taken a hefty "commission." Why would she go after his money and risk raising his anger? But, with the absence of good, verifiable information about her background and the mystery that surrounded her, he could not rule it out.

"I don't think it was her," Yuri said. "The Cayman bank identified the recipient account with a designation that I believe I recognize."

"What was it?"

"The account appears to be one of the old KGB accounts used years ago to fund Soviet operations in the west. I thought that they had been all closed out, but this one appears to have remained open. Its prefix is SU for Soviet Union, and the OIS is for the Office of International Security.

"Mr. Russoff, how much did your friends at the Federal Security Service, or FSB, know about what we were doing?"

Russoff thought a moment. "Well, the organization did lend me two members for my cyber team, and they knew something of my intentions. I do not believe that Nicholas and Rajat are counter agents. They are too young and obviously not trained in that way. Also, they knew nothing about the Cayman Islands account."

"Perhaps the FSB has been tracking your operation secretly and knew much more than we suspected," Yuri suggested. "After all, they have a very sophisticated Internet intelligence network."

Russoff considered this. "I could inquire of them, but they would surely deny it, even if it is true."

In the back of his mind, Russoff still had an uneasy suspicion that Nadia might be behind it. She was altogether too clever, and she remained an enigma—a hauntingly beautiful one.

"I am going to call Nadia and see if she knows anything about this," he said.

Russoff phoned the villa in Porto Cervo and asked to talk to Nadia.

"She is not here, Mr. Russoff," the housekeeper informed him. "The team went down to the port for a celebration dinner last night, and she did not return with them."

Russoff was becoming more agitated. "Let me talk to Slutsky!"

"I think he is out looking for her, sir. He was out most of the night and has not returned. You can probably reach him on his cell phone."

Russoff called Slutsky and wasted no time on pleasantries. "Where is that damn Nadia?"

Slutsky gulped and his voice shook with nervousness. "I absolutely do not know. Last night she was with our group, drinking vodka and celebrating … then the next moment she disappeared. She can't go far. It's a small island and we have her passport, so she cannot leave the country."

Russoff was beside himself. "Idiot! I suspect the passport is fake and the person known as Nadia Pearson does not exist. Slutsky! You screwed up! All of your diligence was wasted on a fictitious person. Official records were probably planted to deceive us. Someone very sophisticated set this up. But was it the Russian Secret Service, Nadia, or some other foreign agency, perhaps the CIA?"

"Sir, I think—"

"I don't care what you think, Slutsky! I'll deal with you later. In the meantime, keep looking for that girl!"

When they checked with the Luxemburg bank, there was no record of receiving the funds, and that account had been inactive for over a decade. The Luxemburg bank officials told Petrovsky that it was possible that the funds had come into the KGB legacy account, and then had been re-routed to another unknown destination. Computer hackers were very sophisticated these days, they said. It was a mystery. Certainly there were individuals in the Soviet intelligence service during the Cold War who would have known about the account and the specifics of its designation. There was also an outside chance that some former CIA operative might have known about it.

Alone in his study in Moscow, Russoff lamented the unthinkable loss. "All that money is gone! It can't have just disappeared into thin air. Where did it go, dammit, where did it go?"

There was no way he would ever know.

In the days and weeks that followed, Russoff would have his security chief, Ivan Slutsky, retrace all of their due diligence in the hopes that there might be some clue as to her real identity. They checked back with Banco Paribas; this time they talked directly with the supervisors in the IT Department. Although the company records showed her employment, none of them remembered her. Their investigation turned to the French State Department and her passport records. It showed the issuance of a French passport to her under her married name, Nadia Pearson, but there were no entries involving any recent international travel other than her departure from Nice to Sardinia.

They inquired of SAIC, only to learn that they had an executive by the name of Jack Pearson. He had disappeared years ago, and they could not release any more information about him.

Slutsky's team visited the apartment in Paris bearing the address on her passport. The landlord confirmed that she had lived there, but she had moved out and left no forwarding address. When they showed the landlord a photo of Nadia, he shook his head and said he could not be certain that his tenant was the same one in the picture. They pressed on with their search, but all of their inquiries led down blind alleys.

She had simply vanished, or perhaps she never existed.

Nadia hated Slutsky. She had decided to "fix him" for good and arranged for some of the money to show up in his account in Moscow. When Russoff discovered that his long-trusted security chief had betrayed him and had perhaps even been part of the scheme to steal his money, Slutsky would disappear ... never to be seen again.

The morning after Nadia had disappeared, Mikhail, Nicholas, and Raj arrived at the tech center to wrap up Project *VedaX*. As the team leader Mikhail had been instructed to download all of the files on the project to a disk set and bring them back to Russoff's corporate headquarters, where they could reverse engineer the elegant solutions that Nadia had brilliantly implemented in building the cyber-attack system.

Mikhail sat down at his workstation and logged on to the system, entering his access code. A message from Nadia appeared on the screen:

> When you read this message, you will know that I am gone. You will never see me again, but I want you, Nicholas, and Raj to know that I have enjoyed working with you and sharing in the success of our extraordinary adventure in cyberspace. You will eventually learn more fully about its outcome. Mr. Russoff may not be happy with the way things turn out and may not reward you appropriately. On the other hand, I do have resources and want to ensure that you benefit from our shared effort.
>
> Go to the cabinet where we keep our supply of blank disks and pull out the one in the seventh slot. Open the case and you will find notes inside that I have left for

each of you. Each note identifies a bank account where I have deposited funds for your use … to make your life a little more comfortable. This is my way of expressing my appreciation for our team effort and the time we spent together in Porto Cervo.
Nadia

"Nicholas! Raj! Come look at this!" Mikhail shouted.

As they gathered around him reading Nadia's message, Mikhail noticed a message flashing at the bottom of the screen:

*After you have read this message, click here for the next step.*

Mikhail moved the cursor and clicked on the button. The screen went blank and the computer shut down. When Mikhail rebooted, all of the files had been destroyed. It was then he realized that Nadia had sabotaged the system.

Back in California, Olga received a communiqué:

*Olga:*

*Mission accomplished! Threat neutralized and all aspects of it destroyed. I have also captured a big prize for us … and I will see you soon.*

*Nadia*

The evening after the $1 billion went missing, Russoff sat alone in the study of his estate near Moscow, reading some documents and taking an occasional sip of a fine cognac. He began to think back to the evening at Antibes and to the extraordinary sexual encounter that he had with Nadia. What she had whispered to him at the critical moment kept haunting him. He increasingly believed that she had really said, "*The game is on.*" The game that he had been playing was the cyber-attack on the US Treasury auction, but had she been *playing him* all along?

It would have been incredibly audacious of her to indicate her intentions in the heat of their erotic engagement. However, he had learned that nothing about Nadia should surprise him.

Perhaps there had been a *game within the game* after all.

# CHAPTER 11

# ESCAPE

It was a warm summer evening on Maddelena Bay as Roberto sat on the aft deck of the *Invictus* enjoying a drink of his favorite single malt whisky, an eighteen-year-old Macallan's scotch. There was not a breath of air that evening, and the water's surface was like glass. It was a rare occasion in that he was there alone, except for a skeleton crew that was nowhere to be seen.

He heard a sound at the swim step at the back of the yacht and rose to investigate. There, rising out of the water, was Nadia, dressed only in a barely-there red bikini. She had swum to the yacht from the beach.

"Can I get a lift to the mainland?"

He recognized the voice on the instant and looked at her. Although she was not blonde, clearly this was the woman that he had known as Tatyana. It was also the same one that he had seen at the restaurant at the Cala di Volpe.

Roberto smiled sardonically. "It will cost you!"

"Can we get underway immediately?" Nadia requested.

He folded his arms across his chest and ambled toward her. "Of course. You know, Tatyana—or whoever the hell you are—I should be angry at you. You took me for $30 million and left me only with the promise of a night together."

"Well, I hear that the deal turned out pretty good for you anyway." She paused and added coquettishly, "And you are going to get lucky tonight. I promise."

Roberto cocked his eyebrows. "Hmm. I think you have promised me that before."

"Tonight, you have me captive," she assured him. "I cannot get away, and I owe you for the passage to the mainland."

"Where would you like to go?"

"Porto Ercole, near Rome."

"Very well then, I will talk to my captain, and we will get underway."

Roberto gave his captain orders to raise the anchor and head to Porto Ercole. It was to be an overnight crossing. There, Popov would meet her and take her to the Rome airport, where she would return to the United States.

Nadia had anticipated this moment and intended to provide him "a night that he would never forget."

But it was to be on *her* terms and *her* initiative ... *not* his.

Soon the anchor was up and the *Invictus* was underway. Roberto was finishing the last of his Macallan's 18 scotch, and Nadia stood at the rail. The forward progress of the yacht created a gentle wind that blew through her wet hair, drying it somewhat. At the cruising speed of the *Invictus*, it would take about twelve hours to complete the crossing from Porto Cervo to Porto Ercole.

"Let's move inside," Roberto suggested to Nadia.

"As you wish."

In the main salon Nadia said, "I need to take a shower to wash the salt water out of my hair and off my body."

"There is a nice shower in the master stateroom, " Roberto said with a clear idea of where that might lead.

"Good, I will see you there." She paused. "Roberto, please ask a steward to bring up an ice bucket and a bottle of champagne ... perhaps Cristal, if you have it?"

"You have expensive taste for a yacht club hostess. Perhaps there is more to you than I know?"

"There is *definitely* more to me than you can imagine."

Cristal was first created in 1867 for Alexander II, the Tsar of Russia. He feared assassination and asked Louis Roederer to commission a Flemish glassmaker to create a clear lead crystal champagne bottle for his prestigious cuvée to replace the dark green bottles. That way he could see its contents; nothing could be hidden inside. The champagne came to be called Cristal as an ode to clear bottle's material.

The master stateroom had a spacious bedroom, a sitting area, and a beautiful marble bathroom. Nadia had finished her shower and was blow-drying her hair when Roberto arrived with the champagne in a bucket of ice. He pulled out the bottle and proudly displayed the Cristal label. He placed it on the end table next to the bed and poured her a generous glass. She pointed to the shower and said, "Your turn."

Through the shower's glass door, Roberto watched as Nadia continued to blow-dry her thick raven hair. The bikini was gone and the pure beauty of her figure was unlike anything that he had seen before. He left the shower and grabbed a towel, partly to dry off his body and partly to disguise his excitement.

Nadia took him by the hand and led him back to the bedroom. "Please lie down on your stomach," she commanded.

This seemed like an unlikely way to commence an erotic session, but he complied. She began to give him a massage.

"This will relieve your tensions," Nadia promised.

Roberto did not have any tensions, but he was full of anticipation. The physical strength and firmness with which she massaged his body seemed contradictory to her small stature and femininity. As she worked the muscles in his back, the feel of her warm hands elevated his pleasure.

She climbed up on the bed and straddled him. She bent down to massage his temples from behind. He could feel her breasts, still somewhat cool from her shower, come in contact with his back. Her derriere rested on top of his and he could feel her legs alongside his hips. This was a very sensual tactile experience.

Nadia then turned him over. He was now facing up as she continued to straddle his body. He reached for her to pull her close.

"No hands!" she scolded him. "Put your arms above your head and keep them there."

This was a very different scene than Roberto expected. Normally he was in control, and his woman was submissive, but Nadia was taking control. Nevertheless, he was excited and highly aroused. Nadia was fully engaged in the act at this point. She ran her fingernails gently across his body, tantalizing him further. He was going crazy. She slid forward, pressing her breasts in his face. The generous size and pink color of her areolas was especially provocative. He kissed her nipples that now stood erect, and then looked into her deep blue eyes.

She bent down and put her mouth close to his ear, with her warm breath flowing on it, and purred, "Are you enjoying this?"

When he began to respond, she placed her finger on his lips and said, "I know."

He could hardly contain himself and keep his arms raised as she had instructed. She slid back down into position and kissed him passionately.

Nadia could feel him accelerating toward a climax.

"I am not ready yet!" Nadia protested.

Roberto was stunned. *What does she mean … "I'm not ready yet?"*

For him there was no turning back. This was the moment to bring this provocative experience to its conclusion. In all his sexual exploits, the woman had always submitted to his timing in an effort to please him. However, in this case, Nadia was in firm control of the process.

She reached into the ice bucket next to the bed, withdrew from him; ice cubes in hand, she grasped his member. This definitely slowed things down. She caressed him and again kissed him passionately. His arousal returned. The pace of her engagement quickened, but in a very controlled way. He could feel her arousal heating up and approaching a peak. She arched her back and flung her arms behind her, supporting her rocking body on outstretched palms. Spasms of pleasure contorted her face, and she moaned her contentment. But then she looked down at him, and a small smile spread across her face. It was an unnerving expression, as if to say, "*I am in charge here!*"

Roberto realized that Nadia was doing this for her own pleasure, not his, adding to his own excitement. This was a fascinating encounter with a very different type of woman. It accelerated to a crescendo and she let out a little gasp … then a scream.

Panting, she looked at him and said,
"*I need another glass of the Cristal.*"

Nadia was awake early the next morning, lying in bed next to Roberto. He was still sound asleep. She could hear the low roar of the engines as the *Invictus* motored toward the mainland. She arose, put on a robe from the bathroom, and walked up to the Bridge Deck and sat in a chair on the deck facing sternward, looking at the long wide wake left by the big yacht as it moved through the sea.

She was soon greeted by a steward, who asked, "Madam, can I get you anything?"

"Some coffee and juice would be nice," Nadia replied. "Also, do you have a secure satellite phone that I could use?"

"Yes, of course, madam."

The steward soon returned with a satellite phone and a continental breakfast. "Would you like anything else, madam?" he inquired.

"Yes, there is another thing. Could you bring me a shirt and slacks from the crew quarters? Perhaps there is a stewardess that is about my size."

The steward nodded. "We have an ample supply of uniforms aboard, so that will not be a problem."

Nadia placed a call to her liaison officer, Anna. It was in the middle of the night back in LA, but Anna was always available to her.

"Has there been anything unusual on the financial news wire about the recent US Treasury auction?" she asked.

"Nothing … why do you ask?" Anna replied.

"I believe that we just successfully pulled off an extraordinary cyber financial transaction that will never be discovered. Our *agency* has $100 million sitting in my Swiss bank account and a $25 million reward due from the CIA. Please let Olga know."

"Consider it done."

"Thanks. Also advise Olga that I will be home soon and share the details," Nadia continued. "I will have an electronic record of the destruction of the cyber threat. Most importantly, I have captured a copy of the software platform that is being used by Russia's FSB cyber warfare unit. I will have some advice for the Treasury Department on how they can beef up their electronic firewall security system. The CIA was correct to be concerned about this threat to America's financial system. Please also set up a follow up briefing for me with the USCYBERCOM team. I will be prepared to provide vital information and technology strategies to deal with the threat."

"That is fabulous, Nadia! There is one other thing."

"Yes?"

"Since, for security reasons, you have been unable to monitor your communications, I have periodically checked your e-mails. You received one from a Mr. Richard Davidson. He said that he had finished his assignment for Senator Wheeler and would like to see you again."

*Davidson?* Nadia reflected fondly. *Ah, the* New York Times *journalist I met during the Wheeler affair.*

"Thank you very much, Anna," she said. "I will follow up on his message in a few days when I return to California."

It was a beautiful summer morning and the Tyrrhenian Sea was dead calm. Nadia rose from her chair and moved to the rail where she could observe the panorama before her. Off in the distance on the port side she could see the island of Giglio. She gazed again at the long wake of white water created by the big yacht *Invictus* as it cut through the blue water.

Nadia watched seagulls passing by and a lone pelican circling above the glassy surface of the sea, looking for just the right fish in the water below. Then, spotting one, the pelican tucked his wings in tightly against his body and plunged like an arrow into the sea, capturing the fish. She was moved by the purity of the whole scene as the morning sunrise swept across the quiet sea.

The forward movement of the yacht created a gentle breeze that blew her raven hair, as if to caress it. She took a deep breath of the fresh salt air, drinking in the full sensual beauty of nature's amazingly rich tapestry unfolding before her. *What a fabulous planet we live on,* she thought.

This was a long way from the poverty and desperation she had known in Bryansk. She felt blessed that a fortunate series of circumstances had taken her life on this journey. It had been Olga's hand on her fate that had brought her here. She shed a tear of gratitude.

She reflected on her emotional progress, starting life as an introverted, awkward waif and blossoming into a confident and resourceful woman of the world. It had begun with Sarah: her first awakening to affection and friendship. The garnet ring had been an extremely generous gift from one that had little to give. The gypsy's spell on the ring had, perhaps, been prophetic in her life. Had it truly protected her from harm? Had it brought her good fortune? She looked down at it once again. She had worn it virtually every day since her departure from Bryansk.

Her friendship with Alexandra had also been an important element in her preparation to explore the domain of affection ... perhaps even romance. The "hug" back in Beverly Hills on their shopping day may have been the turning point. Also, Olga and her colleagues at *the agency* had become like the family that she never had. Mikhail, Nicholas, and Raj had proved to her that men and women could work together, accomplishing extraordinary things, without their friendship being tainted by the complications of romance ... or sex.

Nadia felt ready for more.

Nadia thought back to the men that she had known. She reflected on the night before and the days before that. She wondered where men fit into her life. Now almost thirty, she still had not experienced romantic love. She had not set out to engage in a profession on the dark side of the law, to live a nefarious existence. With this in her background, how could she ever have a normal relationship with a man?

While she had met a number of men that were highly accomplished and affluent, none seemed even close to being suitable. She was beginning to understand her superiority to them intellectually, and that only through the benevolence of kismet—with the ring, perhaps, playing a part too—could she ever hope to meet a man who was truly her peer. Was he out there somewhere? Would their paths ever cross in life?

Her thoughts went back to Richard. While perhaps not her intellectual equal, he was an astute observer of the human condition whose strong opinions, uncompromising integrity, and idealism she admired. More to the point, he had experienced much more than she in life. He had traveled down the road of romantic love and seemed to understand a great deal about it, while she was totally inexperienced in such matters. Experiencing no parental affection as an infant or child, she was a stranger to love. She could learn from him.

For a moment she thought, *If a romantic relationship could evolve for me with any man, perhaps Richard might be an attractive prospect. We had a great time in Napa.* But still there was that little secret of her "work experience" that would surely be a problem for him. Perhaps he was interested. *There was that e-mail that Anna had intercepted.*

Then there was Roberto. Despite his arrogant ways, she had "tamed him" somewhat. He could continue to be a challenge for her ... certainly offering her a relationship with constant dynamic interaction and excitement. That interested her, but still the thought lingered that there might be a better alternative somewhere on her horizon.

She thought about the life that Olga had led as a "loner" and did not want that for herself. Perhaps love would come her way at some point but, for now, she was enjoying the adventure of her clandestine endeavors as an agent in Olga's unique enterprise. Despite her unflattering view of men, Olga was a remarkable woman who had lived, and was living, a rich, exciting life.

Nadia had a growing awareness of the extraordinary gifts that nature had granted her. That good fortune was not to be wasted. She was now in her prime as a young woman and wondered what lay ahead for her. It was a strange life that fate had bestowed upon her.

Soon they arrived at Porto Ercole. The *Invictus* dropped its anchor in the crystal clear, emerald green water of a small bay just outside the harbor. She heard a splash as the anchor was dropped into the water and the clatter of the anchor chain running behind it as it sank to the sandy bottom of the sea. The engines roared in a short burst as the yacht backed down, setting the anchor. On the cliffs above was perched the fabulous Il Pelicano Hotel. Porto Ercole was on a peninsula called Argentario, a summer playground for affluent Italians.

The yacht's tender was lowered to take Nadia ashore. One of the yacht's stewardesses had brought her a shirt, a pair of slacks, and shoes from the crew quarters. Nadia ran her fingers across the embroidered patch bearing the name *Invictus* and smiled. How appropriate it seemed. *The unconquerable—perhaps these alpha males are not as venerable as they think when confronted with a superior female.*

She boarded the tender and as it pulled away, Nadia turned and waved. Roberto looked intently at this marvelous feline creature, unlike any woman he had ever met, and wondered whether he would see her again. He had known her only as Tatyana. He now knew that was not her real name. In San Francisco she always exhibited a serious temperament. Now, she seemed very happy. He wondered why.

His eyes followed the tender intently as it motored toward the harbor and then passed out of sight around the rocky cliffs at the south end of the bay.

He still did not know who she was. But it was clear to him that he had encountered a truly exceptional woman. He wondered, *Who is this mysterious, enigmatic female … this natural beauty with a mind like a Ferrari?*

He was obsessed with the desire to see her again, but had no way to pursue her. It was a strange obsession, for this was the very tigress that had taken a big bite out of him … but surrendered nothing of herself to him. Roberto also thought back to the occasion where he had seen her with the powerful Russian oligarch, Vladimir Russoff. Did this frail tigress have the audacity to take a bite out of him also? It was difficult for him to conceive what had happened.

He was *her* conquest, she was *not his*.

# ACKNOWLEDGMENTS

My deepest appreciation goes to my wife, Twyla, who after reading the first few chapters of this endeavor encouraged me to continue to write. As the book evolved she also became my greatest critic, offering the unbridled candor that only a good wife can.

I want to thank the more than fifty friends that reviewed the sixty-one drafts at various stages of writing this book. They provided valuable feedback that helped refine the story and build out the novel.

I particularly want to recognize Tricia Berns, whose comments at Pelican Hill stimulated the idea for the book. Jennifer Meyers provided especially valuable counsel from the very first drafts. I cannot list them all, but greatly appreciate the review comments provided by all of them.

Thanks also to Amy Trivison for her valuable input on the terrible conditions in Russian orphanages. After a three-week church mission to those orphanages, she was able to provide me with a graphic portrayal of the life of children in those facilities.

Also, I greatly appreciate the continuing advice and encouragement of film producer Alex Rose, who serves on the faculty of Chapman University's acclaimed Film & Media Arts School.

# CREDITS AND REGRETS

I am deeply indebted to the production team that helped me professionalize the book as an end product, including,

My consultant on every aspect of producing the book, Ellen Reid, Ellen Reid's Book Shepherding,

My book designer that made this novel look great, inside and out, Patricia Bacall, Bacall Creative, and

My copy editor, Pamela Guerrieri, Proofed to Perfection.

I regret that I was unable to include the lyrics of the 1950s Harry Belafonte song, *Man Smart, Woman Smarter*, because of the unreasonable demands of the rights holders. These lyrics are fun and relevant to this story. They are widely available on many song lyrics websites … so I recommend reading them.

www.provocateurbook.com